ALL MY FAVORITE PEOPLE

JILL RICE

WILDBLUE
PRESS

WildBluePress.com

ALL MY FAVORITE PEOPLE

This book is dedicated to my daughter,
Miriam Joy Rice Hodges.

Love is not an easy path.
It takes a lot of faith
to endure the journey.
But in the end, love wins.

BAJA CALIFORNIA
SONORA
CHIHUAHUA
COAHUILA
BAJA CALIFORNIA SUR
SINALOA
DURANGO
NUEVO LEÓN
TAMAULIPAS
ZACATECAS
SAN LUIS POTOSÍ
NAYARIT
JALISCO
GUANAJUATO
MICHOACÁN
PUEBLA
VERACRUZ
YUCATÁN
CAMPECHE
QUINTANA ROO
TABASCO
GUERRERO
OAXACA
CHIAPAS

CHAPTER ONE

Present Day

I hate Mexico City. As the capital of Mexico, it is known as the Districto Federal. Mexicans joke that the initials DF stand for De Feo, which literally means "Ugly." I agree with that description. Pollution blankets the Valley of Mexico so heavily that I feel like I am constantly swimming in gritty soup.

Cars left outside overnight are covered in greasy film every morning. On street corners and at stop lights, hordes of young boys, many of them as young as my son, Azul, scramble to clean windshields with filthy rags for a few pesos.

Azul. Dear God, what have I done? Ten minutes ago, I watched this five-year-old boy, my *baby*, walk down the gangplank of the airport jetway to board a plane by himself. When he turned around to take one last look at me, I could see the fear and uncertainty in his eyes. He was terrified. Why didn't I run after him, sweep him and his little teddy bear into my arms, and keep him with me? Why am I sending him away to someone he's never met and who I've hated most of my life?

Because I have no choice. He is not safe if he stays with me.

CHAPTER TWO

Mexico is my adopted country. I gave up my United States citizenship long ago shortly after Álvaro and I married. I love Mexico with its diverse culture and beautiful people. They are my people, *mi familia* now. I pretend I am *pura Mexicana* and that I've never been anything else.

The girl I used to be, raised in Atlanta, Georgia, the cheerleader who was Homecoming Queen and yearbook editor is a distant memory. She is a stranger. When I was seventeen years old, I asked my best friend, Ashley, to take me to the Greyhound Bus Station in downtown Atlanta, swearing her to secrecy. I promised I would keep in touch, but I haven't.

I bought a ticket to Los Angeles, California, the place farthest away from my parents that I could imagine. California is the land of dreams, right? Maybe I could live the life I dreamed of instead of the life my parents wanted for me.

My father, John Gardner, was the senior pastor at Morningside Methodist Church. My mother, Caroline Cassidy, was a psychologist. I have no idea where my father is today, but I've kept up with my mother because she is now a famous author.

Tucked into my son's backpack is a letter to my mother.

Dear Caroline,

This is Azul, your grandson. Yeah, I know, I never told you about him. Add that to the list of things you hate about me.

I need you to take care of him for a little while until I get some things straightened out.

He's a good kid. He loves papaya and pineapple. He likes to look at the stars at night and name the constellations. I'll come get him soon.

His birth certificate is in his backpack. Please keep him safe. He is all I have. Eve.

I try to imagine her face as she reads this letter. It has been twenty-six years since she last saw me. She probably thinks I am dead. Maybe she hopes I am dead, I don't know. Let's just say we didn't have the best of relationships.

CHAPTER THREE

Don't get me wrong. I was not physically abused or mistreated as a child.

I was simply ignored. Neglect, says my therapist, is a form of emotional abuse.

My dad always put God and the church before family. My mother and I were expected to honor "the calling of God" and submit as "handmaidens of the Lord" to his authority. Maybe that's why she eventually left him. She wasn't the submissive handmaiden type.

I was born when my mother was in med school. After getting her MD, she went on to get her PhD in Psychology. Maybe that's why I was more attached to my nanny than to my parents. When my mother started working, and writing books, it seemed like those were her priorities, not me.

However, when it was time to trot me out to make a good impression on a visiting minister or bishop, I was golden for a few moments. "Eve, show Bishop Wilson your latest painting." or "Eve, play *Amazing Grace* on the piano for Sister Carrington." I think John and Caroline truly believed my talents were proof of their consummate skill as the perfect Christian parents.

As a younger child I dutifully allowed myself to be cast into the warm glow of the evangelical spotlight in the hope that afterward, I would continue to be seen and heard. Once I was in high school, though, the moment I was called upon to perform I would make an excuse and lock myself in my room. My mother would furtively whisper through the door, "Eve, open the door now. Don't embarrass your father like this."

I knew I was safe if I didn't respond or open the door. My parents would not dare create a scene in front of visitors. A few minutes later I would hear her cheerfully excusing my absence, "Poor Evie has a bit of indigestion," or other disingenuous untruths.

Eventually, they stopped asking. The house became a cold space to inhabit, the silence filling the corners with longing. The three of us retreated into icy solitude, prisoners of indifference.

CHAPTER FOUR

1997

One thing I do remember vividly about my old life is the fight I had with my mother on the day I decided to run away.

"Mom, why is your suitcase by the door? Tonight is the Homecoming Game and Dance. Aren't you and Dad coming?"

As usual, my mother is in a tizzy, trying to make breakfast, locate her purse, and talk on the phone at the same time. She moves around the kitchen in a frenzy.

"What?" she says to me. She turns back to the phone. "Marci, I'll call you back."

"What did you say, Eve? What about tonight?"

"It's Homecoming." She knows this. It's on the calendar that hangs on the refrigerator. I told her how important this is to me. I've been nominated for Homecoming Queen and tonight the winner is announced.

"Oh honey, that's right. I forgot." She is scrambling to jam a dry piece of toast in her mouth while putting on her coat. A car horn honks from our driveway.

"There's my cab, now. Eve, I'm so sorry. The publisher called yesterday to say she had scheduled me on The Today Show and I'm flying to New York this morning. I'll call you once I get settled in the hotel."

She hurries out the door. No "goodbye." No "I'm keeping my fingers crossed for you." I doubt she has said goodbye to my father. They don't talk much these days. For a minister and a psychologist, they seem awfully screwed up, in my opinion.

The door opens again, and she dashes into the house. I look up expectantly, hoping she realized she had not said goodbye. I move to hug her, but her back is turned, and she is rushing out the door again. "Forgot my briefcase. I'd forget my head if it. . ." The door closes on her words.

Was that the moment the door closed on my heart?

CHAPTER FIVE

I'*m gonna harden my heart.*
I'm gonna swallow my tears.
I'm gonna turn and leave you here.

Jett Patterson, my boyfriend and chauffeur, has the radio in his 1974 Camaro Z28 tuned to WQXI because he hates contemporary music. He has three passions: classic cars, classic rock, and football. I wish I were one of his passions, but it's clear that I'm not.

We've been dating for two years. He's a football player and I'm a cheerleader at The Westminster School. I hate being so cliché, but, well, we are.

I'm belting out the lyrics to Quarterflash's one hit wonder. *I'm gonna harden my heart.*

Jett gives my ponytail a tweak and rests his hand on my leg. "It's a good thing you're so beautiful, Eva, because you can't carry a tune for shit." He slides his hand under my cheerleading uniform until he finds my crotch. *I'm gonna swallow my tears.*

It's kind of a joke that Jett calls me Eva. Last year, we got busted at a bar in Buckhead for underage drinking, so we decided to get fake IDs. One of Jett's teammates knew a guy who lived over an Adult Toy Store on Cheshire Bridge who would do it for a hundred dollars each.

"What's your name sweetheart?" asked the man, a cigarette with burning ash hanging out of his mouth. The odor in the room was stale and stank of beer, sour sweat, and oily machinery. The way he leered at the curve of my breasts in my low-cut slip dress made me uncomfortable. I blurted out, "Victoria Eve Gardner."

He punched some buttons on a machine that looked like a cross between a typewriter, a printing press, and an oven. Clearly a homemade contraption. "Here, put on some lipstick." He handed me a tube of glossy red lip tint. I didn't want to think about how many other girls had used it. "Stand here," he directed. He took my photograph, peered at a screen on the machine and nodded. "Much better. Now you can pass for 21."

The next day Jett and I went back to get our new IDs. I stared at the plastic rectangle. It looked real to me. Obviously, the man had more technical talents than creative ones. "'Eva Victoria?' That's the best he could do?" I scoffed.

"I kind of like that. It's sexy. You are my sultry Latina girlfriend." Jett cupped my breast and traced my nipple with his finger.

I laughed. "Is that how you're going to introduce me to your friends at Ohio State?" Jett had secured an athletic scholarship as a running back and would be heading to college in the fall.

"We'll see each other when I come back at Christmas. You don't need to bother coming all the way to Columbus." *I'm gonna turn and leave you here.*

CHAPTER SIX

The night I was crowned Homecoming Queen was the night I got pregnant. Jett was pretty excited after the game—he broke the school record for rushing and number of touchdowns scored in one game by a running back. A bunch of us went to the bar at the top of the Peachtree Plaza to celebrate both our wins.

"Baby, you are so sexy tonight," Jett whispered. He played with the strap on my Homecoming gown, slipping it off my shoulder and nuzzling my neck. I was embarrassed when the strap broke, and my boob popped out of the skimpy dress. The other players at the table laughed. "Get a room, dawg," one of them shouted.

Jett raised his eyebrows at me. "Yeah?" he asked. I wanted this boy to love me with all my heart.

"Yes," I responded. I wanted to matter to at least one person in my world.

We were both virgins. Up to this point we had engaged in some heavy petting but never went "all the way." Whenever my father preached from the pulpit that premarital sex was a sin, he always made it a point to stare sternly at me and Jett sitting in the front pew.

We were both tired and very drunk that night. After a little sloppy foreplay, Jett climbed on top of me and came almost immediately. When he finished, he rolled over away from me and started snoring softly. I spooned up against his back, filled with such longing that it was painful. I touched myself tentatively. I was very wet and swollen. I rubbed myself until I came.

As I lay beside him in the plush hotel bed, I wondered what "we" would be after having sex. Would he be more attentive to me? Would he introduce me to his family? Did I dare to hope he would propose?

Nothing changed until eight weeks later. We had gone to see *Titanic* right before Christmas. I left the theater three times to pee and once to throw up.

"Are you sick or something?" he asked as we sat in the car in my driveway afterward.

"Something," I said mysteriously, smiling. "I have a surprise for you. I'm pregnant."

The look of total panic on his face brought everything into sharp focus.

"How?" he sputtered. "We only did it once."

I felt tears welling up in my eyes. "I guess once is all it takes when you love someone. You love me, right?"

Silence filled the car like a noxious gas. I opened the car door, leaned out, and vomited again.

The next day he handed me $500 in cash and said he would drive me to "take care of it."

"Let me think about it."

"Think about it?" Jett's voice rose but he remained calm. "Eve, I have a career in football ahead of me. The scouts are saying I could go pro by my junior year. There is no 'thinking about' it."

I put the money in my purse and walked away without a word. That night, I packed a small duffle bag, left a note for my parents on the kitchen counter, and asked Ashley to drop me at the bus station.

"What'll I tell your parents if they ask me where you are?"

"I don't even know if they'll care." Obviously, they would contact the police when I went missing, after checking with Jett and Ashley to see if I was with them.

I imagined they would be furious with me for bringing a scandal home to Reverand Gardner and his wife, the famous self-help book author. *A pregnant runaway! What kind of parents must they be?* They would be the talk of the church, enduring the congregation's furtive whispers and sideways glances for months.

That thought brought a smile to my face.

CHAPTER SEVEN

T he bus smelled like body odor and greasy gas station pizza. I filled a barf bag before we ever pulled out of the station.

I stretched out, my back against the window and my feet propped up on the seat to prevent swelling. Even though I was only eight weeks pregnant, my body was revolting against this invasion. I had constant headaches and heartburn from the beginning and now, fat ankles.

I was such a hypocrite. I was furious with Jett for not wanting this baby, but I wasn't sure I wanted it either. Being a teenage mother was never the plan I had for my future. I excelled in art classes in high school and had taken private lessons at the High Museum. When I was awarded a scholarship to the Savannah College of Art and Design, I dreamed of being the next Georgia O'Keeffe.

I looked around at my fellow passengers. I had never been on a bus before, except for a school bus. The lady across the aisle from me had two toddlers in tow, neither one of them wearing coats or hats to guard against the late December cold. Dressed in a thin coat herself, she had wrapped them in knitted blankets. The two men behind me were loud and obnoxious. They kept kicking the back of my seat, asking if I would like some company. I considered turning around and throwing up on them. Or at least dumping my barf bag in their laps.

The man in front of me smelled nice. I leaned forward to fill my nostrils with the green woodsy scent of his cologne. It smelled like the one my dad wore. Earl Grey Flannel, or something like that. The man was youngish, maybe in his early twenties, and was reading a book in Spanish.

I considered starting a conversation with him. I had taken two years of high school Spanish. *Hablas Espanol?*

Duh, obviously he did but I was too tired to engage him. Besides being sick most of the time, I was also constantly tired. I closed my eyes, trying to ignore the noise of the fussy toddlers and the bothersome idiots behind me.

"*Señorita*? Miss?" Someone shook me awake. It was the man in the seat in front of me. "We've stopped in Birmingham to pick up more *pasajeros*." He pointed to my brown paper sick bag. "May I throw that away for you? Would you like for me to get a Coke to settle your stomach?" I reached into my coat pocket and pulled out a dollar.

"Oh no, no, *Señorita*. Allow me. It is my treat." I wondered if his nice guy demeanor was an act and if I would soon have to fend off his advances.

"*Señora*?" He turned his attention to the woman with the children, who had quieted down and were asleep on her lap. "May I bring you a coffee and perhaps a chocolate for your *ninas*?"

I loved the way he said chocolate. *Sho-co-lah-tay.* It sounded so elegant.

The man was not my type. He looked about as tall as I was (5' 8") and was very thin. Long black curly bangs framed his face. I liked big blond football players. Like Jett.

Jett. Would he miss me when he found out I was gone? Would he be sorry he didn't get on his knees and ask me to marry him?

Suddenly reality set in. I was one hundred and fifty miles from home. My only identification was a fake driver's license in the name of Eva Victoria, with a fake address in Stone Mountain. If something happened to me, no one would know.

I was completely alone and on my own.

The man returned with my soda and noticed my tears. "*Qué le pasa, Señorita?* What's wrong? Are these men bothering you?" He handed me the cup and stood in the aisle by their seat. When he spoke, it was a command. "Move to the back of the bus, *chamacos*." One of the men uttered a protest but stopped abruptly when the man opened his jacket slightly and nodded to his belt.

I've never seen two people skedaddle so fast. They settled into the last seat on the bus and did not speak to me for the rest of the trip.

CHAPTER EIGHT

The man had purchased two travel pillows in the bus station, one for me and one for the mother. She accepted the pillow gratefully and propped her head against the window.

Warily, I accepted the pillow. He settled into his seat and turned around. "My name is Álvaro. Álvaro Castillo. Have a pleasant evening, *Señorita*." Within a few minutes he was fast asleep.

The mother caught my eye and we smiled at one another. She put her hands together in a prayerful motion and looked up. I nodded my head. It seemed we had a guardian angel.

I slept fitfully, waking several times to go to the bathroom. The men in the back of the bus ignored me.

About 9:00 the next morning the bus pulled into the station in Shreveport, Louisiana. The driver announced a one-hour layover, which would be enough time to get breakfast and stretch my legs.

I walked around the exterior of the bus station. It was clear but cold. The brilliant blue sky lifted my mood a bit. Until I thought about my mother, knocking on my door this morning, and finding my bed made and unslept in. She would call Ashley first and then Jett. Panicked, she would wake up my father. What do you know—they will be forced to have a real conversation for once. *Where is our daughter?*

Through the window I saw Álvaro seated at a large table. The mother and her two daughters were seated with him. He motioned for me to join them.

Suddenly, I was ravenous. I ordered eggs, bacon, pancakes, and a Coke. The little girls ordered pancakes, making a buttery syrupy mess all over the table and themselves. One of them laid a sticky hand on Álvaro's jacket. He leaned in to hear the little girl's whispered question and then laughed. "No, I'm not an angel in disguise." He pronounced it "ahn-hell."

My curiosity got the best of me.

"What gives, Álvaro? Why are you being so kind to strangers on a bus?"

"If you must know, *Señorita. . .*" I stopped him right there.

"I'm Eva." I turned to the mother. "What's your name?"

"Jessica." She gestured to her daughters. "And this is Emily and Alexis."

"Nice to meet you," I said.

"*Encantada*," said Álvaro, nodding to all of us. "As I was saying, Eva, you remind me of my younger sister, Maria Luisa." He offered a smile. "My mother raised me to treat all women as I would like for my sister to be treated."

Jessica looked at Álvaro like he was the second coming of Jesus Christ. I was slightly less enthusiastic and suspicious of his motives.

"How old are you, Álvaro?"

"Twenty-three."

"Where are you headed?"

"Acapulco. I have relatives there."

"Are you going for a visit or to stay?" For the briefest of moments, I saw a shadow cross his face.

"I will be living in Acapulco for a while," he said stiffly.

It was apparent Álvaro did not want to answer any more of my questions. He laid his napkin on the table and stood. "Ladies, *con su permiso*." He dropped a fifty-dollar bill on the table for the waitress.

When I boarded the bus again, Álvaro was sitting in my seat by the window. He motioned for me to sit beside him. He cocked his head toward mine and spoke in a low voice. "I apologize for being rude at breakfast. I want to explain my situation."

As he shifted his torso, his jacket fell open and I got a look at what it was that scared the men into submission last night. I wanted him to explain his situation, too. He had a gun tucked into his waistband.

He began hesitantly. "I am a *contador*."

Shocked, I exclaimed, "Gross! You're a bull fighter?"

Álvaro laughed so hard he choked. "No! That's a *matador*! I'm an accountant."

I raised my eyebrows. "You need a gun to operate an adding machine?"

"For what I did for El Tiburón? *Sí*, I needed a gun."

CHAPTER NINE

It took a full 24-hour day to reach our next stop, El Paso, Texas. For a good part of the trip, Álvaro and I shared our stories. He used a lot of Spanish words, but I got the gist of what he was saying.

"El Tiburón, you've heard of him, no?"

I nodded my head. Who hadn't heard of Pedro Luis Salas, nicknamed 'The Shark,' the biggest drug kingpin in Mexico?

"I worked for one of his lieutenants, Hector Garcia. He was responsible for the distribution of drugs on the east coast.

"I was Hector's *contador*. I kept one set of books for Hector," Álvaro paused, "and under Hector's direction, another set of books for El Tiburón.

"Everything was fine until last year. Hector got greedy. He took a lot more *dinero* off the top. When Pedro Luis came to me and asked about it, I had to make it clear my loyalty was with him. I told him about the two sets of books."

I listened with lurid fascination. My suburban middle-class upbringing sheltered me from contact with people like El Tiburón. And from people like Álvaro, for that matter.

"Two days ago, I killed Hector Garcia for El Tiburón. He promised he would protect me and reward my *fidelidad, my loyalty*. But when I got home, I found my sister, Maria Luisa, hanging from her bedroom ceiling.

"Whether it was El Tiburón's men who killed her or Hector's, I don't know. I didn't wait to find out."

Had I heard the man correctly? Did he just admit he had murdered someone? And then, his sister had been murdered in an act of revenge?

I didn't know what to say to someone whose life was marked by this kind of violence. "I'm so sorry," I said lamely. "What will you do in Acapulco?"

"I have a place to hide out."

"How long?"

"How long what?"

"How long do you have to hide from El Tiburón?"

"Para siempre, chica. Forever."

CHAPTER TEN

It was in El Paso that Álvaro planned to rendezvous with the bus that would take him to Acapulco.

My bus was scheduled to leave for Los Angeles in two hours. Álvaro and I ate a burger together at the bus station grill. I was feeling queasy, so I didn't eat much. Álvaro asked if I felt unwell. I lied and said I was fine.

After lunch, Álvaro lingered as long as he could before boarding the Estrella de Oro south into Mexico.

He gave me a long hug by the side of the bus. "Take care of yourself, Evita," he whispered and kissed me on either cheek, like I've seen Europeans do in the movies.

I watched him climb the steps and find a seat. The bus sat idling while the passengers' luggage was being loaded. The diesel fuel was making me sick, so I waved and ran to the bathroom.

As I was running, I felt a gush between my legs. By the time I made it to the bathroom, I was doubled over in pain. A whole lot of blood and other gross stuff poured down my leg. "Somebody help me," I whimpered.

"Eva? Is that you?"

It was Jessica's voice coming from inside a stall. "Hon, are you OK? What's wrong?"

"I think maybe I just had a miscarriage."

The door to the stall banged open. Two little girls peered around the stall, open-mouthed at the carnage on the floor. "Stay there," Jessica ordered. "Where is Álvaro?"

"He just left on the bus to Mexico."

Jessica flew out the door. Emily, Alexis, and I stared at each other. "Stay right there, girls," I said. One of them started to cry. "It's ok, baby, it's ok. Mama will be right back."

The cramping was so strong that I sank to the floor, crying, and writhing in pain. Alexis and Emily were both crying now and calling for their mama.

For one brief moment, I silently cried for my mama, too.

CHAPTER ELEVEN

I must have passed out because the next thing I remember is Álvaro bending over me, wiping my face with a warm cloth.

Gently, he lifted me from the floor and helped me settle onto a bench in the ladies' room.

Jessica corralled her terrified children and shooed them out of the restroom. She had a bus to catch.

A Greyhound employee entered as they were exiting, "Do I need to call 9-1-1, folks?" she asked as she surveyed the mess on the floor.

"Yes," said Álvaro.

"NO!" I said forcefully. "No, I just had a heavy period and didn't make it to the toilet in time. I'm sorry about the floor. I'll clean it up."

"No need, darlin.' I'll get the cleaning crew."

"You need to see a doctor," said Álvaro after the woman left.

"No, I can't. I don't want anyone to know where I am."

"Anyone as in your parents? Don't you think they are worried about you? And the baby?"

"They don't know about the baby. If they did, they would disown me."

"You are too weak to get back on that bus today. Would you allow me to get a hotel room for you and we'll see how you feel in the morning?"

The cramping had begun to subside. I nodded. "Where will you sleep?"

"I'll get a room near yours. Let me get your bag off the bus so you change into clean clothes."

Álvaro brought my bag and stood outside the door while I changed. "Shout if you start to feel faint or dizzy," he said. "I'm right here."

I cleaned the blood off my legs with paper towels and threw away the blood-soaked clothing. I wiped my shoes as best I could. I had only brought one pair with me.

The bathroom had a vending machine for feminine hygiene products, so I bought a few sanitary pads in case I kept bleeding.

Álvaro had called a cab and directed the driver to take us to the nearest motel. I could see the driver's smirk in the rear-view mirror. It occurred to me he must think I was a prostitute.

I laid my head on Álvaro's shoulder in the backseat of the cab and sobbed. What had I been thinking when I ran away? I had no plans. I just did what I always did— overreacted on the spur of the moment without thinking or planning.

As soon as I felt well enough, I would go back to Atlanta and face the consequences.

CHAPTER TWELVE

Álvaro passed on the first three motels the driver took us to. They were old and run down. Álvaro declared them *peligroso*. I was thankful. They looked pretty dangerous to me, too. Álvaro instructed the taxi driver to take us to a Marriott hotel.

At the front desk of the Airport Marriott, he paid for two adjoining rooms. He carried my bag to my room and unlocked the door. Handing me my key, he said, "I'll be right next door. Are you hungry? We can order room service."

"I would like some soup, please."

Thirty minutes later, a waiter knocked on my door with a tray. Three kinds of soup, a football-shaped roll with butter, and a Coke. Closing the door, I heard Álvaro knocking on the adjoining door.

"Is everything to your liking?"

I was getting used to his formal English. At first, I found it ridiculously old-fashioned, but I was warming up to it.

"It's perfect," I said, unlocking the adjoining door. "What did you order?"

"Tamales, beans, and rice. Would you care for a taste?"

Álvaro carried in his tray and set it on one of the beds. "How are you feeling, Eva?"

"Better. I took a nap and some Tylenol."

"Still bleeding?"

"Not so much. I don't want to talk about it with you."

"If you won't see a doctor, then we are going to talk about it. Are you running a fever?"

"I don't know."

Álvaro moved to the bed where I was sitting and placed his hand on my forehead. "No fever. *Bueno*. A few days in the hotel and you will be strong enough to travel again."

"I. . .I'm not going to Los Angeles. I'm going back to Atlanta."

Álvaro was silent for a while. Then, "Is that what you want to do?"

"God, no, but I didn't plan this well and I don't have a place to live or a job once I get to LA. I was being stupid, and I overreacted. I was scared to tell my parents about the baby. So, I ran away."

"How much money do you have?"

Oh shit. Was this how it ended for me? Robbed and left for dead in a hotel in El Paso?

Álvaro must have read the panic on my face.

"Oh no, *no te preocupes*. Don't worry. I'm just asking because, *tú sabes,* I'm an accountant. I help people start businesses and make money. I could help you if you wanted.

"You could help me start a business and make money? Doing what?"

"It depends. What are your interests? What do you like to do?"

"I like art: painting and sculpting. I had a scholarship to an art school next year." I laughed. "I guess that's over with. I've painted a few tee shirts for friends. I've made beaded jewelry. I like being creative."

Still a little suspicious of this man and his motives I asked, "Why would you help me? You don't know me. Why are you doing this?"

"Maria Luisa was pregnant when she was killed." His eyes filled with tears. "I couldn't save her or her baby, but maybe I can help you."

He picked up his tray and carried it into his room. "Good night, Evita." The door closed but he didn't lock it on his side.

I put my tray outside the door, turned out the light, and crawled under the covers. A few minutes later, I crept over to the adjoining door and cracked it open.

I slept restlessly and startled at every thump and bump in the hotel. Several times I heard the door creak open and felt Álvaro stand beside my bed. He'd put his hand on my forehead for a moment and then go back into his room.

CHAPTER THIRTEEN

Hours before daylight, I heard Álvaro stirring in the other room and the muffled sound of a television tuned to a news station. After a while, he peeked into the room and saw I was awake.

"May I enter, Evita?"

"Sure." I had slept in my clothes since I hadn't thought to bring pajamas with me.

"The police have found Hector Garcia's body. And Maria Luisa's. They are looking for me in connection with both killings. El Tiburón is taking care of *cabos sueltos*."

"What's that?"

"Details. *¿Cómo se dice*, loose ends? I am a loose end. I need to cross over into Mexico this morning."

"Oh." I was surprised at the wave of sadness that washed over me. I had only known Álvaro for four days. He was a stranger in every sense of the word. Why did I suddenly feel so panicked that he was leaving?

"How are you feeling this morning? Are you still. . ." he hesitated, knowing I was embarrassed, "bleeding?"

"Only a little bit. I'm feeling better."

Someone knocked on the door and said, "Room Service."

Álvaro approached the door with a gun drawn and peered through the peephole. Satisfied, he tucked the gun into his pants and pulled his shirt over it.

"*Pase,*" he said as he opened the door.

He paid the waiter and pulled the cart to the edge of the bed. "I ordered my favorite breakfast. Huevos rancheros, tortillas, frijoles, and fruit." I watched as he tore the tortillas into large pieces and used them like a spoon to pick up his eggs.

He acted as if it were normal to answer a door with a gun in his hand. I felt a slight shiver of fear. I should have wanted to distance myself from this criminal, but I was fascinated by him.

Was the fear and panic I felt because I was afraid of Álvaro? Or was it because I was afraid of going back to my family in Atlanta?

I picked at my breakfast and then packed my duffle bag.

"We'll take a taxi back to the bus station. I'll make sure you are settled on the bus to Atlanta before I board my bus to Mexico."

"No." I shocked myself as well as Álvaro.

It occurred to me I was making one of those dramatic and totally immature decisions that my seventeen-year-old self made all the time. "Can I go to Mexico with you?"

CHAPTER FOURTEEN

Álvaro was silent for a long time. Too long. I feared his answer would be "no."

I pled my case. "Last night you said you would help me start a business." I pulled a wad of bills out of my purse. "Look, I have almost two thousand dollars I can give you." For several years I had saved every penny that came my way—birthday and Christmas gifts, babysitting, and of course, the $500 Jett had given me for the abortion.

"Keep your money, Evita."

So that's it, I thought. The answer is no.

"You realize that I am a wanted man. The FBI, El Tiburón, they are all looking for me. You are in danger when you are with me."

"That didn't stop you from befriending me on the bus. Where was all your concern for me then? Just go ahead and admit it, I'm too much trouble."

Álvaro burst into laughter. "You are not trouble. You were my cover. I was safer when it appeared I was traveling with you. The authorities are looking for a single man of my description, not a couple."

"So, you were *using* me? Oh my god what a. . ." I let loose a string of profanity that would have gotten me grounded for three months if my father had heard it.

Álvaro was amused by my outburst. "*Ay, tú eres una leona.* You are a lioness. *Qué bueno.*"

I tapped my foot impatiently. "Was there a 'yes' in that mumbo jumbo?"

He simply nodded and held out his hand. "*Vámanos.*"

CHAPTER FIFTEEN

It was only when we boarded the Estrella de Oro bound for the border and Mexico that I realized I had lost track of time. Every passenger on the bus had armloads of Christmas presents.

"Is today Christmas?" I asked.

"No, it is *La Noche Buena*, the day before."

Christmas Eve. My family cooked a big feast on Christmas Eve, exchanging gifts with my grandparents, aunts, uncles, and cousins. We would play games and sing Christmas songs. My dad always ended the evening with the Christmas story from the Bible. I thought about Mary, who would have been a little younger than me, far from home, giving birth to a baby of questionable parentage in a shed.

I had never really found God or Jesus to be useful but thinking about Mary ignited a little spark of hope in my heart.

When we reached the border to cross into Mexico, we got off the bus and walked through customs. "Let me do the talking," Álvaro instructed. "You are my girlfriend. We are going to Acapulco where I will introduce you to my family. We are only staying one month. One month. Anything longer will raise concerns. Understand?"

I held my breath as the Mexican customs officer checked our driver's licenses and asked Álvaro a few questions. The officer never once addressed me. After a short interview we were back on the bus and on our way south.

CHAPTER SIXTEEN

I am ashamed to admit that I had envisioned the entirety of Mexico being like spring break in Cancun. Sunny days, piña coladas, beautiful hotels, and lush tropical landscaping.

Northern and central Mexico were much different than the coastline. It was scrub, dirt, and cacti for mile after mile. When we stopped for lunch in Chihuahua, Álvaro brought me a bowl of a stew called *pozole*. I was savoring the earthy taste of it when I noticed the lady cooking it in a huge iron cauldron over a roaring fire. She was stirring it with both hands, and I nearly fainted when she lifted a goat's head out of the pot, with eyes, hair, and teeth intact. Then she stirred it back in.

The bus stopped for the night in Torreon. We were now deep in the heart of central Mexico. At a small hotel adjacent to the bus station, Álvaro paid for two rooms. "Go freshen up, and then meet me in the lobby in thirty minutes for dinner."

I showered under a trickle of tepid water and then had to dress in my travel-worn clothes. My blue jeans were filthy, and my tee shirts were rank with body odor.

A knock at the door startled me.

"Eva, it's me."

I opened the door. Álvaro handed me a large shopping bag.

"I thought your clothes might be a little dirty, so I got you a few things at a store down the street. If they don't fit, we can take them back. I'll wait for you downstairs."

He had chosen a flowy dark skirt and a long-sleeve white top. The blouse was beautiful; it had a peasant neck and puffy sleeves. Colorful flowers were embroidered around the neckline. A leather belt studded with silver and turquoise, and a woven wrap were also in the bag. My Doc Martens completed the outfit.

"*Muy bonita,*" Álvaro said when he saw me.

"I will pay you for these," I said. "Everything fit perfectly. Thank you."

We walked a short distance to an open-air restaurant.

Álvaro ordered for me, since I could not read the menu. "No *pozole*!" I said, laughing.

The food was delicious—garlicky steak and a salad of avocado, tomatoes, and onions. Since I hadn't eaten much of the *pozole* at lunch, I finished every bit of the *carne asada* and *ensalada de aguacate.*

"You get your first Spanish lesson tonight," said Álvaro. "Repeat after me: '*la comida está muy rica.*' The food is very tasty."

I repeated the words and was pleased when Álvaro complimented me. "You have a very nice accent. I think you will pick up Spanish very easily."

Although I had taken Spanish in school, the limits of my vocabulary were apparent. And understanding the rapid-fire barrage of Spanish that came at me—forget it. I was clueless and entirely dependent on Álvaro to communicate for me.

After dinner we walked around the city square, which was called a *Zócalo.* There was a large oak tree in the center and from it hung hundreds of lighted snowflakes.

Even though it was very late, throngs of people were milling about. There was a mariachi band playing lively music. People were dancing, lovers were cuddling on wooden benches, and a clown made balloon animals for children.

At midnight, the bells in the tower of the church on the square rang out, piercing the darkness with a beautiful melody. "*Feliz Navidad!*" people shouted to one another, hugging and kissing their loved ones.

Álvaro gave me a brief hug and said softly, "*Feliz Navidad*, Evita." He withdrew from his pocket a small gold box with a white ribbon.

I opened the box. Inside was a small pendant on a delicate silver chain nestled on white satin. Two hearts, one large, one small.

"A small remembrance, for you and the little one you lost. Merry Christmas." Álvaro told me much later that the necklace had been intended as a gift for his sister. She was murdered before he could give it to her.

That night, I fell in love with Mexico and Álvaro.

CHAPTER SEVENTEEN

T he next morning, I bought a Spanish-English dictionary at the bus station. By the time we stopped in Querétaro for the evening, I had driven Álvaro crazy with hundreds of questions about pronunciation and grammar. But I had a much better understanding of the language.

At dinner, I asked if I could order for us. *Arroz con pollo* wasn't that hard to order and I did a passable job conversing with the waiter.

Later we walked around Querétaro's *Zócalo*. There were many revelers celebrating Christmas and Álvaro linked his arm with mine to guide us through the crowds. When we reached our hotel, I asked if we could sit by the outdoor fire pit. "I need to talk to you."

As we were being seated, I asked the waiter for a glass of wine from the local vineyard. Álvaro ordered one, too. I sipped the wine slowly, savoring it. The next day was my eighteenth birthday, but I didn't tell Álvaro. Honestly, I felt much older. In retrospect, I realize it was the maturing that takes place as we stretch ourselves beyond our self-imposed borders and embrace new cultures and experiences.

"What is your plan? How are we going to live? Are we safe from El Tiburón?"

"So many questions, Eva. My plan? *Bueno*, we are going to live in Acapulco. I have a camper in a park on the edge of a lagoon. It is very secluded. We will be safe there.

"But first I must take a detour to Taxco. I have money and other things in a safe deposit box that I need to retrieve in person. I don't trust anyone else to do it."

"Taxco?" I opened the map of Mexico I had purchased along with the dictionary. "Oh, near Mexico City."

"Taxco is an old silver mining town. It is very charming. Lots of steep narrow streets and quaint architecture. And many jewelry stores."

"How will we pay for things? Will you work?"

"I was paid very well by El Tiburón and Hector. If we live modestly, neither of us will have to work."

"I can't do that. I won't be dependent on you. I need to earn my own money."

"Fine. We'll figure that out."

The wine was making my head fuzzy. "I need to go to bed." I giggled. "I'm feeling the wine."

Álvaro walked me to my room. "Good night."

I leaned in and kissed him. Softly at first and then with passion. I felt every nerve in my body fire with electricity and my knees felt a little weak. Álvaro broke our embrace.

He looked directly into my eyes and smiled. He had a beautiful smile. "*Buenas noches,* Evita," and he pushed me inside my room and shut the door.

CHAPTER EIGHTEEN

I heard Álvaro unlock the door to his room next to mine. I was ashamed that I had propositioned him. It was obvious he did not have the same feelings for me that I had for him. The last thought I had before I fell asleep was, "He really *is* a nice guy."

The next morning, of course, I apologized for my behavior. Álvaro waved his hand dismissively. "No problem. I have already forgotten it."

On the bus to Taxco, I thought about what I could do to earn money to support myself. At home, in Atlanta, I babysat the children of people in our church. I had a summer job in a little boutique in Ansley Mall. But language was a problem for me in Mexico. It would take a while for me to be fluent in Spanish. Defeated, I retrieved the dictionary from my duffle bag and immersed myself in study for the remainder of the trip.

CHAPTER NINETEEN

We arrived in Taxco after dark, and I sank into the hotel bed, exhausted and weary. Traveling cross country by bus was all I could afford. I wondered why Álvaro, who seemed to have plenty of money, had chosen not to fly.

When I asked him, he said there were too many of El Tiburón's operatives in airports, especially the larger international airports like Atlanta. He would have been easily recognized. He had intended to ride the bus to Birmingham and then fly to Acapulco from there. But when he met me, he realized the cover I offered him was the better option.

The sun woke me early as it was rising over the mountaintops. I gazed out the window and gasped. I had a full view of the city—the white buildings with red tile roofs nestled in the valley and on the mountain slope. To this day it remains the most breathtaking view I've ever seen.

Below me on the cobblestone streets little white Volkswagen Beetle taxis zipped around the hairpin curves and jockeyed for position in the narrow alleyways. I had a view of the *Zócalo* and the Basilica Santa Prisca, an amazingly ornate church I couldn't wait to explore.

"Álvaro!" I exclaimed at breakfast. "Please let's stay a while. It is so beautiful here and I want to explore this city."

Álvaro smiled slyly. "If you can ask me in Spanish, we'll stay as long as you like."

I dug out my dictionary. "*Por favor, podemos quedarnos en Taxco? Es una ciudad muy hermosa y quiero…*" I had to look up the word for explore. "Oh, that's easy, *explorarla.*"

Álvaro applauded my effort, "*Muy bien hecho*, Evita."

"I'll be back later this morning. I have business to attend to." He laid a business card and a stack of pesos on the table.

"Here is the hotel business card. If you get lost, ask a taxi to bring you back here. Have fun."

Ordinarily I might have panicked at the thought of being left alone in a foreign city, but I was strangely exhilarated.

First, I perused the flower stalls near the *Zócalo*. Fresh blossoms of every variety were lined up in clay pots for a city block. The explosion of color made me dizzy with delight. Walking a little further down the street, I found the city market. There were straw hats and baskets, colorful pottery and tiles, and beautiful embroidered clothing. The vibrancy of color and beauty was too much for the artist in me. I stood in the middle of the market and cried tears of joy. I felt like I belonged here.

Álvaro was not exaggerating when he said Taxco was the silver capital of Mexico. Every other store window gleamed with handmade jewelry and works of art in silver. I was fascinated by the process of casting liquid metal and hammering sheets of silver into these intricate and delicate designs.

In an art supply store, I bought art pens and paper. Holy crap! Álvaro had given me one thousand pesos! (I realized later that was just a little over a hundred dollars, but still. . .)

The smell of coffee at a little sidewalk café lured me in and I stopped to enjoy a *café con leche* and one of those football shaped rolls (which I learned is called a *bolillo*) filled with cheese and ham. I sat there for hours, drawing everything in sight. La Santa Prisca. A terra cotta pot filled with flowers sitting beside an ornate ironwork garden gate. A little girl wearing a straw hat, petting a cat in her lap, her face beaming with love.

My favorite drawing from that afternoon was a statue of The Virgin Mary. She was quickly becoming my favorite saint.

I was amused by the thought of having a favorite saint. The concept of God was not foreign to me, but neither was God personal to me. God was just a mean old man who put a lot of restrictions on my life by way of my parents' interdictions. "That movie is not appropriate for you." "That dress is too revealing." "You can't go to the sleepover because we have church the next day." I had no use for such strict oversight.

The expectations that were foisted upon me as the daughter of a minister, not only by my parents but by the parishioners, were onerous. I had longed to be free of religious restrictions. Here, in Mexico, I was untethered. It felt *delicioso*.

The deepening shadows on the sidewalk outside the café and the chill in the late afternoon air made me realize I had tarried much longer than I intended. As I hurried back to the hotel, I hoped Álvaro wasn't worried. I found him in the bar talking to a police officer. When he saw me, he leapt up and ran toward me. I could see the relief in his face. He lifted me off the ground in an embrace so tight I couldn't breathe.

"*Querida*, where were you?"

He turned to the police officer. "*Aquí está mi esposa, gracias a Dios*." He tucked a thousand peso note into the officer's hand.

The police officer smiled and addressed me in English. "*Señora*, you had your husband quite worried. I am thankful you are safe." He touched his hat in a small salute and left.

"Oh, so we are married, now?" I teased Álvaro.

He ignored my question. "I've been looking for you for hours." Álvaro wasn't angry; he was genuinely concerned that I had gotten lost, or worse.

I opened my sketchpad. "I had the most glorious afternoon." I showed him the pages of pen and ink drawings.

He took the pad and flipped through it. "These are remarkable. You are a very accomplished artist. I had no idea you were so talented." He smiled but the anxiety had not yet left his eyes. "I was so worried. Did you get lost?"

"No, I didn't get lost. I went to the flower stalls and the city market. I walked all over town. I talked to people, and they were so kind to help me when I didn't understand what they were saying. It was a magical day."

"Eva Victoria, you are full of surprises." The way he looked at me made me think he was seeing me in a new light.

CHAPTER TWENTY

Álvaro was pensive throughout dinner. I thought perhaps he was still upset. "Are you mad at me?"

"Mad? No, I was not angry with you." He reached over, took my hand, and gave it a squeeze. "I was worried."

I held on to his hand, turned it over and traced the lines on his hands with my fingertips. Peering closely, I said, "Ahhh...I see you will live a long and prosperous life. Hmmm, you will have six children and, oh, no, that one's just a freckle. You will only have five children."

He laughed, and drew my hand toward him, caressing it with both hands. He kissed my palm softly, and then my wrist. My body trembled with desire.

"Álvaro," I said, but he placed a finger over my lips.

"You have a beautiful life ahead of you, Evita. Don't waste it on me."

"But I've never met anyone like you, and. . ."

He shushed me quietly. "Because you are so young. Of course, you haven't experienced many lovers."

"Yesterday was my birthday." I searched for the correct words. "*Yo tengo deciocho años.*"

Álvaro was stricken. "Your birthday?" He motioned for the waiter's attention. "We'll have a cake to celebrate."

I waved the waiter away. "It's not cake I want for my birthday."

CHAPTER TWENTY-ONE

I leaned over and whispered in his ear. I made it clear what I desired for my birthday.

"No, we cannot. It is too soon after losing the baby."

I was crushed. The man had made it clear over and over that he did not want me. I rose from the table. "I'll see you in the morning."

I was crying uncontrollably by the time I reached my room. A few minutes later there was a knock at my door. "Eva? Evita?"

I didn't answer.

"Let me explain."

"Go away." I said through my tears. "I won't bother you again."

"I will not have this conversation in the hallway. *Por favor*, open the door."

When I opened the door, Álvaro was holding a beautiful bouquet of flowers that had been hastily wrapped in paper and tied with twine.

"Did you steal these flowers from the market?"

He shrugged. "Maybe. Now listen to me. Your body is not ready to take a lover. You had a miscarriage a week ago."

"Fine. I understand." My voice was monotone. "Thank you for the flowers." I gestured for him to leave.

Álvaro sat on my bed. "*Querida*, you do not understand. I desired you from the moment I met you."

I looked up, surprised.

"*Sí, mi amor.* There is something in you that calls to me, like a twin to my own soul. You are the woman I want to spend the rest of my life with."

He pulled down the sheet and blanket on my bed. "Come. Tonight, I will hold you, nothing more. Tomorrow, we will visit the doctor."

Álvaro undressed himself and then undressed me. He stood before me in his underwear, thin and wiry, shaking like a leaf in the wind.

I was just as nervous. We tucked the covers around us and held each other. We didn't even kiss. There was a calm and peaceful stillness that surrounded us. It was probably because of the season, but the song, "Silent Night, Holy Night" played over and over in my mind. We fell asleep and spooned together. *Sleep in heavenly peace.*

CHAPTER TWENTY-TWO

Álvaro was gone when I woke up but the bed on his side was still warm. The pillow held the slightest fragrance of his cologne.

I felt a soul connection to Álvaro, and I believed he felt it, too. So, *this* is love, I thought.

I showered, dressed, and was about to leave the room when he opened the door. He kissed me and handed me a *café con leche* and a *gallina*, a yummy cream-filled pastry.

Neither of us spoke as we ate our breakfast. It was almost as if we knew the mystical spell from the evening before could be broken with the wrong words.

"Eva, *te quiero*. I love you." He took a tiny velvet bag from his jacket pocket. He removed a wide silver band sprinkled with tiny diamonds. "Will you marry me?"

Is it possible to fall in love with someone in eleven days? I don't know anything about this man except that he used to work for a drug cartel, and he likes huevos rancheros. All he knows about me is that I was impregnated by my high school boyfriend, and I tend to throw fits when I don't get my way.

We are from different cultures. We speak different languages. We are miles apart in so many ways.

"*Querida*, we speak the same language—the language of love. We are '*almas gemelas*,' twin souls. And we are not miles apart. We are here together, in this moment, because we were destined to fall in love."

In my brief eighteen years, I had never met a man as kind and wise as Álvaro. He is generous and thoughtful. He is crazy about me. And I am enchanted by him.

Of course, I said, "yes."

CHAPTER TWENTY-THREE

On New Year's Eve, we were married in a small church with a dirt floor and rustic wooden pews. I wore the skirt and embroidered blouse Álvaro had bought for me in Torreon and the silver necklace he had given me Christmas Eve.

A large wooden statue of Mary stood behind the altar. As we stood before her and made our vows, I sensed her loving arms reaching out to bless our union.

Our marriage was purely symbolic. We would not be legally married for a few more weeks. There were several hoops to jump through before being married by a magistrate. But in the years that followed, we always celebrated our anniversary on December 31st, the day we committed to love one another forever.

That night, we had room service delivered to my room. We opened the windows wide and watched the New Year's Eve fireworks in the *Zócalo* light up the night sky. I could sense Álvaro was as nervous as I was about sex. I wasn't sure if he had had relations with a girl before, but my only experience had been once with Jett. Although it was only three months ago, it was a distant unpleasant memory.

As the fireworks reached a crescendo, I leaned over and put my head on his shoulder. When he lifted my chin and kissed me, an intense desire sparked within me. I was barely eighteen years old and completely inexperienced, yet I felt passion rise and take over.

I had heard my father preach against lust. I wondered why. Lust combined with love was an incredible feeling. Shouldn't this be the level of commitment and devotion and sexual attraction that all couples should strive for?

I eagerly stripped Álvaro of his clothes. In my haste and passion, I ripped more than one button off his shirt. I remained clothed as I began to explore his beautiful perfect body. How had I ever thought this man was not my 'type'?

I kissed his neck and felt him tremble. I was worried that I wouldn't know how to make love to a man, but it seemed as if his body was telling me what it wanted. I kissed his chest and then his stomach. He was hard between my breasts. Should I. . .?

Álvaro yelped several times with pleasure and when I was finished, he was drained. But he held me tightly, nuzzling my neck and whispering, *"Te amo, mi amor. Te quiero, mi vida"* again and again.

His hand slipped under my blouse and caressed my breast. The difference between how it felt when Jett had touched me and Álvaro touching me now was stark. Jett touched me to satisfy himself. But Álvaro? This man touched me to satisfy *my* deepest longings and desires. This man had nothing but my pleasure on his mind.

Álvaro lifted my skirt over my hips and slipped off my panties. When his mouth touched me, hot and wet, I ascended into heavenly realms. I screamed in passion so loudly that the someone in the next room banged on the wall and yelled, *"dale, dale."*

"What does that mean?"

"'Dah lay'" loosely translated means, 'go for it.'" Álvaro and I collapsed in laughter.

CHAPTER TWENTY-FOUR

1998

I convinced Álvaro to abandon the idea of going to Acapulco to live in a camper. I had been completely charmed with Taxco and wanted to put down roots. We rented a house one block from the *Zócalo*, a little stucco cottage with a red tile roof and a huge courtyard garden.

We spent the first few weeks of January taking care of legal matters. My sole identification was a fake driver's license in my fake name. It turns out you can get almost anything in Mexico with enough *plata.* It took less than two weeks and every penny of my two thousand dollars to get a fake U.S. birth certificate and passport in the name of Eva Victoria.

We were married on January 15, 1998, in the magistrate's office.

After we married, I obtained a legal driver's license and passport in my married name, Eva Castillo. I also applied for Mexican citizenship.

The doctor had advised me to wait three weeks after the miscarriage to have intercourse. We satisfied each other every night during the waiting period, but we were both anxious to join our bodies together physically.

The night we were married in the courthouse, Álvaro dragged our mattress into the gazebo in the center of our courtyard. We encircled the mattress with candles. Lights twinkled in the trees and shrubs around us. Two *chimeneas* warmed the chill of the evening air.

Álvaro opened a bottle of champagne and unwrapped a small cake from *La Pastelería*. He poured two glasses of champagne and handed one to me. "I will love you and cherish you forever," he whispered, kissing my neck. He lowered the strap of the shimmery satin nightgown I had selected for our special night. "Many waters cannot quench love; neither can the floods drown it."

"That's beautiful. Is it from a poem?"

"Of a sort. It is from the Bible. The Song of Solomon." He nuzzled my breast.

Álvaro took his time kissing every inch of me. My body ached for him, and I was delirious with desire. When I couldn't wait any longer, I spread my legs and pulled him into me. When he entered me, I sensed the mystery and magic of our two bodies uniting as one. I had never felt anything so sacred in my life.

I met every thrust with equal passion and when we came together, there were tears in both our eyes.

We wrapped ourselves in blankets and lay entwined together. I don't know where it came from but another verse from Song of Solomon floated through my consciousness before I fell asleep. *I am my beloved's, and my beloved is mine.*

CHAPTER TWENTY-FIVE

I spent the first few idyllic months of our marriage learning to cook, improving my Spanish, and creating art. Having no real responsibilities, I would gather my pens, gouache paints, and paper every afternoon for a foray into town. Álvaro usually accompanied me, spending the afternoons with a *café con leche* and *pan dulce* at our favorite bakery, *La Pastelería.*

One day as I was drawing La Santa Prisca, a woman stopped to observe me. I paid her little attention; tourists often stopped to comment on my work or ask directions. I was able to converse in Spanish with great ease and proficiency by now and few people recognized me as an American.

She asked if I was a local artist or a tourist. "*Yo vivo aquí,*" I replied. I live here.

Her name, she said, was Adela Torres and she owned a gift shop around the corner. She liked my drawing and painting style and inquired if I had a portfolio to show her.

We set an appointment for the next day to visit her at La Paloma, her shop. Álvaro and I hurried home to take my drawings and paintings off the wall and sort them into a professional presentation.

Sleep eluded me that night. When I left Atlanta and abandoned my dream of attending the Savannah College of Art and Design, I didn't think another opportunity for me to develop as an artist would ever come along.

"*Ya ves, mi amor,*" said Álvaro, bringing me a cup of chamomile tea to calm my nerves and help me sleep, "you see, my love, what is meant for you will not pass you by."

Álvaro had more confidence in my talent than I did. It is very difficult for an artist to view their work with an uncritical eye. We see every line that could be straighter, or every color that is just a tiny shade off. It is rare that an artist is ever one hundred percent satisfied with their work.

My nerves were all jangly the next morning. Álvaro arranged my artwork in a portmanteau, and we walked the few blocks to La Paloma.

My hand trembled as I reached to open the beautifully carved wooden door. Álvaro placed his hand atop mine. "*Querida*, I have faith in you. Trust yourself."

Adela was all smiles as she showed us around her shop. It was really more of a gallery—several local artists exhibited their work in La Paloma. There were intricately woven shawls, watercolor and oil paintings, magnificent majolica pots and tilework, and hammered copper kitchenware. And then there was the silver. Some of the most renowned Taxco silversmiths were represented. The jewelry was exquisite; many of the pieces encrusted with precious gems. There were silver goblets, platters, and objets d'art, too.

Álvaro and I sat with Adela in her office. She studied my artwork carefully and I could see she was impressed. There were a few small pieces that made her gasp.

"*Eva, el arte suya está magnifico.* Your art is magnificent. Of course, I would like to represent you." She peered over her glasses at me. "Tell me, why didn't you bring your silverwork?"

I was confused. "I don't understand."

She handed me a few small pieces of paper, the ones that were the cause of her exclamations.

In his haste to gather my art together, Álvaro had inadvertently included some sketches I had made of silver jewelry designs.

"Your ideas are very different. I would love to see your work in silver."

I explained to Adela these were mere sketches, little more than doodles, and that I was not a silversmith.

"You should be a silversmith. These designs are incredible."

I was stunned. I was in the silver capital of Mexico and an art dealer was telling me that my silver jewelry designs were incredible.

Adela handed me a card. "Can you meet me here at 3:00? I would like to show these to Alberto Morejón."

Alberto Morejón? He was only the most famous of the famous silversmiths in Taxco.

CHAPTER TWENTY-SIX

T he meeting with Alberto Morejón was a momentous turning point in our lives.

His charisma and presence were enormous. He had a big booming voice and his large frame towered over me and Álvaro. I felt like a tiny dwarf planet about to be sucked into the orbit of a supergiant star.

"I am impressed, *Señora*, by your sketches. You have a unique approach to design. Have you worked in silver before?"

"No. I really was not aware of it as an art form until I came to Taxco."

Morejón chuckled. "Our ancestors have been creating art in silver for millennia. Creating sacred and ceremonial objects in precious metals is part of our indigenous heritage. Your perspective on *milagros* is distinctive. The combination of sacred and natural charms is a fresh take on the genre. I think we can create a niche market for your jewelry."

I knew that *milagro* means 'miracle' in Spanish. I wasn't sure what that had to do with my silver designs. He must have seen my confusion because he asked, "Where are you from, Eva?"

He was surprised when I said I was from Georgia. "*Ah, Los Estados Unidos. Por eso usted no conoce los milagros.*" The United States. That's why you don't know about *milagros.*

I was pleased that he thought I was Mexicana, but the fact that I was not explained why I had no idea that *milagros* are small charms and religious iconography made from various metals. Each charm symbolized a prayer or a wish.

"They originated in ancient Iberia and were introduced to our ancestors by the Spanish Catholics in the sixteenth century. Traditionally they are used to petition for a miracle or as an offering of gratitude for a receiving a miracle or blessing." Morejón took a keychain from his pocket and showed me the small charm depicting The Virgin Mary superimposed over a heart. "Like this. When my wife was sick, I prayed with this *milagro* every day."

I had sketched a bracelet with charms in various shapes: a hummingbird, peace symbol, angel wings, ankh, compass, and heart. I didn't think I was doing anything radically different.

My sketch was reminiscent of my mother's charm bracelet when I was a small child. When I was fussy, she would take it off and let me amuse myself with it. I loved the jingly sound it made when I shook it. That sound has always reminded me of my mother.

I had drawn the bracelet because I was hoping to find a local *platero*, silversmith, who could make it for me.

I had also sketched a necklace with similar charms— fairies, flowers, leaves, a dragonfly—that dangled from a piece of leather studded with silver beads.

The pièce de resistánce, though, was something entirely different. In many of the shops throughout Mexico I had seen pictures and sculptures of *Quetzalcōhuātl*, the Aztec god. Depicted as a plumed serpent, he is the god of life, light, and wisdom.

I modernized *Quetzalcōhuātl's* shape, with softer rounded edges. I drew his feathered headdress a bouquet of colorful plumage, studded with inlaid semi-precious stones.

"This," said Morejón, "is exquisite. Your style is groundbreaking. Señora Castillo, I would like for you to apprentice with me."

In that moment, I sensed a shift in my destiny. It literally felt like a physical movement, the tooth of a gear shifting one notch over and creating a completely new and different trajectory.

Who controls our destiny? My father would say our lives are predestined, that a supremely powerful God has fixed all events and outcomes. Deviation from the master plan is not possible. I never believed that, and my father and I argued about it more than once.

When I boarded the bus bound for California and met Álvaro there were two distinct possibilities. One is that was the master plan for my life all along, and a divine being conspired to make it happen. Or, two, our lives are a series of millions of random choices and occurrences, our path constantly shifting away from one direction toward a different one. Every day, the destination changes.

I'm not a philosopher. I don't know which is true. I only know that when I shook Morejón's hand and accepted his proposition, I was certain all my choices had led me here.

CHAPTER TWENTY-SEVEN

Señor Morejón was as friendly as he was imposing, and he immediately drew Álvaro and me into his inner circle. He invited us to his home for dinner that evening. He lived a few streets over from us, so we picked up a bottle of wine and desserts downtown and walked to his home.

His housekeeper, Aurora, made a simple meal. *Mole poblano* and *empanadas de calabasa*. The flavor of chicken with mole is bold. A rich red sauce made with chilis, onion, nuts, seeds, and chocolate, one either loves it or hates it. I loved it! The pumpkin empanadas were delicious. I had never eaten either dish before that evening. I asked for three helpings and a cooking lesson from Aurora.

Señor Morejón, or Beto, as he asked us to call him, gave us a tour of his home. It was much like ours, a small two-story bungalow with cool terracotta floors, white stucco walls, and colorful Talavera tilework in the kitchen and baths. Most of his furniture was the heavy colonial wood that is typical with older generations in Mexico, but I noticed a difference in Beto's. He had painstakingly carved out channels and divots in the furniture and filled each crevice with silverwork or crushed turquoise mixed with resin.

His collections of traditional Mexican folk art were displayed on the walls and flat surfaces. I was looking at a print of Frida Kahlo's work and Beto took it off the wall for me to examine. It was not a print. The back of the canvas was smudged with paint, and I could make out the faint outline of words in pencil. *"Regresa a mi"* and a sketch of the broken heart that was painted on the front of the canvas. I imagined the painting and the message, "Return to me," referred to the tumultuous relationship between Frida and her husband, fellow artist Diego Rivera.

"The Kahlos were neighbors. They lived across from our family home in Coyoacán. Our parents were good friends." Beto took the painting and looked at the back of the canvas. "Frida and Diego were star-crossed lovers." He smiled. "They were renowned for their wild parties. That's where I met William Spratling and eventually, I became his protégé. I have Frida to thank for that."

I had picked up a silver bowl on the buffet in Beto's dining room and noted the interlocking 'WS' stamped on the bottom, indicating it was one of Spratling's earlier pieces. Although he was American, he is known as the "Father of Mexican Silver." I had visited the Museo Guillermo Spratling in Taxco which housed his personal collection of Mesoamerican artwork and his own silver designs. Beto's house was just as interesting, if not more.

It was dark when Álvaro and I walked home. It was a clear night and the stars winked at us in the cloudless sky. "*Mira*, look," he said, pointing. "It's El Cisne."

"What's that?" Álvaro was an amateur astronomer. He often disappeared late at night and I would find him in our courtyard with his telescope trained on the heavens.

He traced the shape of the constellation with his finger. "Cygnus. The Swan: see her swimming through the Milky Way? This is a good omen, *querida*. She is a symbol of good fortune and prosperity." He drew me to him and kissed me. "And, swans are associated with the goddess *Afrodita*."

It took me a minute. "Oh, Aphrodite. The goddess of love." We stood in the middle of the street in a tight embrace. A taxi swerved around us on the narrow street. "*¡Dale!*" the driver shouted, laughing.

I pulled my husband down the street toward our house and had his shirt unbuttoned before he could get the gate unlocked. We left a trail of clothes on our front walkway and the porch.

CHAPTER TWENTY-EIGHT

My apprenticeship with Beto began at 8:00 a.m. sharp. We adhered to a strict schedule with a mandatory break at 10:30 a.m. with coffee and *pan dulce* served by Aurora. We would work until 2:00 p.m. and then break for siesta. Employees would come back at 4:00 p.m. for another couple of hours of work. Beto, however, ended his workdays at 2:00 p.m.

Beto was a widower whose children were grown and living in other parts of the world. He had lived in Taxco all his adult life and was the most famous silversmith in town. After siesta he would wander around town, taking a *café* with one set of friends, a *postre* with another, and dining around 9:00 p.m. with a third group. He was the life of every gathering.

But with me, he was a tough taskmaster. I was the last apprentice he would take, and he pushed me to achieve not only his level of expertise, but to love the process he considered a metaphor for the transformation of the human soul.

"Silver is a goddess—the energy of the moon. Using your own intuition and skill, you will transform a common chemical element into something extraordinary and magical."

He picked up a sheet of copper. "We start with copper first."

I was disappointed. I wanted to jump right into working with silver.

"Silver is a precious commodity. You will make a lot of mistakes in the first few months. You will work with copper because it is much less expensive than silver.

"Draw a simple design on the copper. I will show you how to cut out the design with a saw and file the edges until smooth. Tomorrow you will wash, solder, and polish it." He placed the tools on my bench: a saw, various blades, bees wax, and a file. And goggles. "Never work without wearing goggles," he admonished. He pointed to a scar on his eyebrow. "One sliver of metal to the eye and you can be blinded."

Using a permanent marker, I drew a dove on a piece of copper, then its wing, and a tiny heart. He showed me how to determine the proper blade and load it into the saw. I coated the blade with wax and began to saw. The copper immediately flipped out of my hands and landed on the floor.

Beto shrugged. "It happens to everyone."

My hands ached after holding the copper sheet in one hand and gripping the saw in the other. Several times my hand slipped, and I cut the side of my forefinger. I noticed the other silversmiths wore fingerless gloves to protect their hands.

After about an hour, I had the bird cut out. The edges were very rough. Beto handed me a metal file.

"File in one direction only, away from you." He watched me for a moment. "No, no, this is not a saw. Smooth strokes, like you are playing the violin."

It did not take as long to smooth the edges. Aurora rang a bell indicating it was time for the coffee break. I was feeling frustrated because it had taken so long to saw and file one small shape. The other silversmiths gathered around my bench and provided much needed encouragement.

"*Se ve bien, chica.*" It looks good, girl.

"*Muy bien hecho.*" Very well done.

I stole a glance at Beto. He had a proud look on his face. My heart swelled with joy. I didn't know it at the time, but Beto Morejón would not only become my mentor, but he would be the father Álvaro and I had been searching for.

I still have the necklace I made that day. It hangs on a strip of leather from the rearview mirror in my car. I touch

it every day and whisper a prayer of gratitude to La Virgen
that I have created the kind of life I had always wanted.

CHAPTER TWENTY-NINE

For five years I worked with Beto as an apprentice. I learned every aspect of silversmithing. Sawing, filing, cutting, hammering, shaping, and polishing. I learned lost wax casting and became proficient at carving various substrates in which to cast liquid metal. I spent tens of thousands of hours honing and perfecting my skills.

Under Alberto's tutelage, I became an accomplished silversmith. My designs won awards from the *Asociación de Plateros,* the association of silversmiths. I was making a name for myself throughout Mexico as his protégé and heir.

In 2003, Alberto retired. I couldn't blame him. For fifty plus years he had bent over a bench, working with 6000-degree flames to refine and shape silver.

"My mission is complete. *El manto te pasa a ti.* The mantle is passed to you."

I was twenty-three years old and a nationally recognized silversmith. I was more than ready to spread my wings and soar.

And soar we did. It is amazing what a talented artist and a brilliant accountant can accomplish together. I handled the creative end and Álvaro's financial acumen shepherded the business from a small local gallery into an international wholesale jewelry firm.

We were a dynamic team. The business grew steadily and eventually we employed over one hundred people in our workshop and warehouse. In 2017, I "retired" from the jewelry bench. I had twenty-eight young eager silversmiths hammering out my designs every day.

I turned my attention to fulfilling one of Álvaro's most fervent wishes. We had tried for years to get pregnant, but it never happened. We had come to terms with being childless;

we were so much in love with each other and the life we had created that we were completely content without children.

At least I was content. I could tell Álvaro felt his life wasn't complete without children. He would ogle babies in shops and in the *Zócalo*, playing peek-a-boo with strangers' children. Whenever any of our employees had babies, he would encourage them to bring the little ones to the studio and Álvaro would play with them all afternoon.

Secretly, I was thankful I didn't have children to divide my attention. I am certain I would have failed a child as deeply as I believed my mother had failed me.

During the years that we were building the business, taking it from a local concept to an international corporation, I was ambitious and singularly focused. I recognized the dilemma my mother faced, trying to complete graduate school, build a business, and write books, all the while taking care of a young child. I finally admitted to myself that I probably would have made the same choices she did. A little seed of forgiveness toward my mother took root in my heart.

CHAPTER THIRTY

Present Day

I t is hard to reconcile now, and I am ashamed to admit it, but whenever I thought about what my parents must have been going through since my disappearance, I immediately pushed the thoughts away. I live with tremendous guilt for not contacting them once Álvaro and I settled in Taxco.

Why did I stay silent all these years? The longer I maintained the estrangement, the easier it was to pretend I had never been Victoria Eve Gardner. I told myself that my parents were glad I was gone and that they would not welcome me back. I think that was the only way I could deal with the shame that haunted me.

Unforgiveness inhabited my heart, weighing it down with heavy sorrow. I often visited the rustic church where Álvaro and I made our commitment. I would sit in the front pew and talk to Mary. She would gaze at me through her carved wooden eyes and gentle smile, and I felt her love and acceptance. *"Perdónate,"* she would whisper into the silence of the sanctuary. "Forgive yourself." But I couldn't.

I was usually in the church alone, as it was on the edge of town and not nearly as popular as the ornate Santa Prisca. One day, an elderly nun shuffled through the church and genuflected at the altar. She ignored me and walked down the center aisle. A moment later, I heard the rustle of her habit skirts, and she sat in the pew beside me.

"What is troubling you, my child?" Though she wasn't a priest, and I wasn't Catholic, I made my confession to her. When I finished my story, she took my hand, and I felt a jolt of electricity shoot through me. "You followed the path that led you to your destiny. *Perdónate.*" She touched my abdomen and smiled. "You will have a son," she said, "with eyes as blue as the heavens."

I didn't know what to say. I was in total shock. I muttered, "Thank you, Sister," and she rose to leave. When I got up to leave a few seconds later, she was nowhere in sight.

I like to believe that little old nun was actually my favorite saint, La Virgen Maria, come to life just to comfort me. In Mexico, there are stories of Mary sightings in almost every town.

Álvaro, who had been raised Catholic, was skeptical. "Those are folk tales. People drink too much mescal and think they see visions of saints and devils."

When our baby was born, Álvaro exclaimed over his beautiful blue eyes. "How is that possible? I have brown eyes and you have green eyes. His eyes are *azul*."

"Azul," I said thoughtfully, as my newborn son nursed. "This little fellow's name is Azul. He is a gift from heaven."

CHAPTER THIRTY-ONE

After Azul was born, we put together an escape plan. Álvaro knew there was a decades-old bounty on his head. As long as it was just the two of us, we knew we could flee quickly with little preparation. But a child changed the dynamics of safety and survival.

We bought property outside of Taxco, where there were many naturally occurring caves in the mountainsides. Our property had two caves. We outfitted the largest cave with a generator, extra clothing, water, non-perishable food, and medical supplies. Every six months, we replenished the supplies and charged the generator. This would be our "safe house" in case circumstances prevented us from leaving the area right away.

We kept a small bag with cash, passports, keys, and important documents at the ready. It was our "earthquake bag," the bag we would grab every time a *temblor* shook our area. Every Taxqueño home had an earthquake bag. Ours was also our escape bag in case Álvaro was recognized and we had to disappear at a moment's notice.

Each night we packed the bag, wondering if we were being overly cautious. After all, many years had passed since Álvaro had betrayed El Tiburón and killed Hector Garcia. It was possible the bounty had been cancelled after such a long interval, but we had no way of knowing for certain. We decided it was better to be safe than to gamble with Azul's life.

CHAPTER THIRTY-TWO

Two days ago, Álvaro came home from *La Pastelería,* as frightened as if he had seen a ghost.

After all these years it was still his favorite afternoon pastime to have a *café con leche* downtown and people watch. Most of the time Azul and I joined him, but today Azul had a swim lesson and Álvaro had gone alone to the café.

He entered the house, locked the door behind him, and drew the curtains. "I saw someone today I recognized from *Los Guerreros.*" This was the cartel operating in our area of Mexico. So far, we had successfully avoided contact with any of the local criminal organizations by paying hefty *morditas,* bribes, to the police officers and government officials in Taxco.

I felt sick to my stomach. "Who was it?"

"Mario Villa. I knew him in Atlanta. He worked for El Tiburón and the Morelia cartel." Álvaro's voice trembled. I could tell he was worried. "He works for *Los Guerreros* now."

"Did he recognize you?"

"I don't think he saw me."

"What should we do?"

"Get our affairs in order. We leave for Canada tomorrow afternoon."

Through a shell company Álvaro created that was untraceable back to us, we had purchased a house on Vancouver Island in British Columbia. It was the second part of our escape plan. First, we would hide out in the cave until it was safe to travel. Then we would make our way to Canada under new identities.

The next morning, I took Azul to school as usual and then stopped by the business. When Azul was born, we had hired a manager, and she ran the business very efficiently. It would be in good hands. There was paperwork filed with our attorney that would turn the business and profits over to our employees in the event of our deaths or disappearance.

I made certain everything was in order with the warehouse and showroom. I approved a few new designs and made some changes to a piece our top silversmith was working on. I met with Ximena, the manager, and she gave me a few documents for Álvaro's approval. I signed off on them. Before I left, I gave her a hug. "We are so thankful for you, Ximi. See you tomorrow." Before I left, I put my cell phone and personal computers in a drawer in my office.

I picked up Azul from school and headed home to get Álvaro. He had stayed home to pack a few things and get the house ready for our absence.

The first thing I noticed when I parked our car on the street in front of the house was the iron gate was unlatched and open. We *never* leave the gate open.

"Zuzu, stay in the car for a minute. I'm going to run in and get my bag and we'll go to the playground."

I cautiously climbed the tile steps to our house. The front door was unlocked. We *always* lock the front door.

I nudged the door open with my foot. I didn't hear any noise inside the house. "Álvaro?" No answer. I opened the door a little wider.

There was blood everywhere, splattered on the walls and floor of the living room. The rug in the entry way was soaked.

We had a prearranged plan. The priority is to protect Azul. If one of us is killed, wounded, or kidnapped, the other leaves with Azul and gets him to safety. We solemnly promised each other there would be no deviation from the plan, no heroics to try to save the other. We take Azul to safety. We stay with him. He is the priority.

I reached around the door frame and frantically felt for the escape bag. It was right where we had left it the night before. I grabbed it and ran back to the car.

"Mami! Can we get ice cream before we go to the playground?"

I kept my voice as cheerful as possible. "Oh, I wish we could, Zuzu, but I have a surprise. We are going on a little trip!"

"Where's Papi? Is he going with us?"

"No, *mi amorcito,* it's just us."

Azul frowned. "Will he meet us later?"

A sob rose in my throat. "I hope so, *mijo*, I hope so."

CHAPTER THIRTY-THREE

The drive from Taxco to Mexico City is less than three hours. I kept an eye on the road behind me the entire time, looking for any vehicles that might be tailing us. I didn't think we were being followed but as a precaution, I drove fifteen kilometers past the airport exit and then doubled back.

As soon as Azul saw the signs for the airport, he asked, "Are we going on an airplane?"

"Yes. You are going to visit your grandmother in Atlanta."

"I have a grandmother! I didn't know that." The innocence of my boy brought tears to my eyes. He was the only one in his school class who didn't have grandparents, aunts, uncles, and cousins nearby, which is uncommon in Mexico. When asked about family by friends or acquaintances, Álvaro and I would just smile and say, "It's just the three of us" and deflect any other questions.

At the airport, I bought a single one-way ticket to Atlanta and walked him to the gate.

I withdrew the envelope with Azul's birth certificate, passport, and a letter to my mother from the escape bag and zipped it into his backpack.

I knelt and hugged my son. "Azul, I need you to pay attention to what Mami is saying. This is very important."

I took his teddy bear from his backpack and placed it in his arms. "You and Chico are going on the plane without Mami. There are nice ladies on the plane who will take care of you. I'm going to find Papi and then we will come get you at your grandmother's house."

Azul's lower lip trembled, and his eyes filled with tears. "I don't want to go without you, Mami. *Tengo miedo.* I'm scared."

"I know, *mijo*, but the ladies on the plane will take care of you. Now, listen carefully." I showed him the envelope in his backpack with my mother's name on it. *Caroline Cassidy*. "Give this to the lady who walks you off the plane, OK?"

He nodded solemnly.

It took all my strength and resolve to put him on that plane. I watched him walk down the gangplank and as soon as he boarded, I sat on the bank of chairs outside the gate and wailed.

I touched the two hearts on the little necklace that Álvaro had given me so long ago. For the first time in twenty-six years, I prayed. Not to God. But to the one who touched my heart long ago. I said a prayer to La Virgen Maria. Who better to entrust my son to than a mother who knew the pain of being separated from her own son?

CHAPTER THIRTY-FOUR

Where is Álvaro? Is he dead? There is certainly enough blood in our living room to indicate he could be.

Was he kidnapped by El Tiburón or Los Guerreros? Would the kidnappers contact me for ransom?

Is he wounded? If so, is he hiding in the house? Should I go back and look for him? Had he escaped and gone to the cave as we planned?

The plan. No heroics. Get Azul to safety. Stay with him.

I said another prayer. "Álvaro, wherever you are, please forgive me."

CHAPTER THIRTY-FIVE

Álvaro's passport, new identity documents, and some of our cash were missing from the escape bag. I believed it could only mean one thing—that he had escaped and made it to the cave as planned.

I left the airport and headed for our mountain property. I could not risk going back to our home or our business location in case a home invasion had taken place and my movements were being tracked.

It took about two hours to reach the point where the road ended. I continued the rest of the way on foot. The cave was a little more than a mile up the mountain. There was not a trail or path cut to the cave because we wanted to discourage unwanted visitors. So far, our cave had not been discovered by the hikers and rock climbers who frequently trespassed our property in the lower elevations.

The sun had set, and it was a rough climb. I used a compass and a flashlight to navigate up the hillside and remain on course. The terrain was extremely rocky and covered with scrub. What would have taken an hour and half in daylight took me over three hours. It was after 10 pm when I reached the cave.

I stumbled over a pile of rocks at the mouth of the cave and let out a string of curses. Deep in the recesses I heard my beloved Álvaro laughing at me. He switched on a flashlight. "*Querida,* why are you here?" He reached out his arms and embraced me. "Where's Zuzu?" He looked around. "Where is our son?"

For the first time ever, my husband raised his voice at me. "Eva! Where is Azul?"

"I put him on a plane to Atlanta. To my mother."

Álvaro inhaled a deep long breath. He leveled his voice. "And why did you not go with him?"

"I couldn't leave you. What happened at the house?"

He ignored my question. "What is your mother's phone number? I want to make sure my son arrived safely."

"I don't have my mother's phone number. You know that. I have had no contact with her since I was seventeen."

"Have you lost your mind? You sent a five-year-old on an international flight alone without arranging for someone to pick him up? He must have been terrified. What were you thinking?"

I was sobbing. "I don't know. I sent Azul to my mother for safety. But I just couldn't leave you."

"Eva, if you had just followed the plan…we talked about this. You promised."

Álvaro wasn't looking at me. He was typing on his cell phone.

"Who are you calling?"

"I'm googling your mother's phone number. I have to know my son is safe." He was silent for a moment. "Ah, *aquí está*."

It was after midnight in Atlanta, but my mother answered the telephone. "Hello, this is Cal. Who the heck is calling so late?"

"Señora Cassidy, this is Álvaro Castillo. I am Azul's father. Is he there with you?"

"Danny, it's Azul's father! Let me put you on speakerphone."

"Is my son with you?"

"Yes, don't worry. He is here with me and my husband, safe and sound. He is asleep now."

Álvaro had put the call to speakerphone as well. I felt a tug in my heart as I heard mother's voice.

"Can you tell me what is going on? Are you safe? Is Eve with you?" My mother's voice broke when she said my name. "I was so worried when I read her letter. Where are you?"

Álvaro held out the phone to me. I shook my head and mouthed, "No."

"*Señora*, Eva is fine, she is safe. She is not here at the moment, though."

"Oh. . .ok. . .would you tell her. . ."

I could hear my mother sobbing and a man in the background comforting her.

"Would you tell her I love her, and I never stopped looking for her. Tell her I'm sorry. So sorry."

"Yes, I will." Álvaro offered the phone to me again, but I turned away.

"Señora Cassidy, we will fly to Atlanta tomorrow. Tell Azul that Papi and Mami are coming to get him."

"I will tell him. If you'll let us know your arrival time, we will pick you up at the airport."

"No, we will hire a car. I will let you know our arrival time. Goodbye, *Señora*."

When Álvaro ended the call, he broke down and cried. I tried to put my arms around him, but he turned away.

"*Mi amor,* forgive me. Please forgive me."

His response gutted me.

"What kind of mother are you? You are not who I thought you were."

CHAPTER THIRTY-SIX

I still did not know what had happened at our house. Had there been a confrontation with Mario? If so, how had Álvaro escaped unharmed? It was clear I would not get any answers tonight. Without a word to me, he walked to the back of the cave, laid down on an air mattress, and switched off the flashlight.

It was pitch black in the cave. The moon was just a sliver in the sky and did not provide any ambient light. I fumbled for my flashlight, turned it on, and found a stack of blankets. I laid two blankets on the ground as a pallet, made a pillow with another one, and covered myself with a fourth one.

A few hours later, I was shaken awake. "Shhhhhhh, be quiet," Álvaro whispered. "One of the trip wires I set up was activated. Someone is coming."

I sat up, alarmed.

He gave me his handgun. "Go to the back of the cave. No matter what happens, stay hidden."

Álvaro peered out of the mouth of the cave and over the ledge. "They are close. I see a flashlight."

I retreated to the back of the cave. He sat on the blankets where I had slept.

We waited.

It was impossible to approach the cave with any stealth. There were too many dried branches, leaves, and loose rocks littering the way. I heard the climber stop outside the cave. Then, I heard the sound of a rifle being cocked.

"I know you are in there. I tracked your cell phone. Thanks for making that call tonight. If you hadn't, I would have never found you up here."

"Mario, how nice to see you again." Álvaro stepped forward and faced his old friend.

"Imagine my surprise when I saw you in town, *un fantasma del pasado*. A ghost from the past. El Tiburón was very excited, too."

"*Cuanto?*" Álvaro asked. I knew what he meant. He was asking Mario how much El Tiburón was offering for his capture.

"*Tres millones. Dólares.*"

Three million!

Álvaro laughed. "I can give you that tonight, Mario. Come on, *hermano*, we go way back. Don't let the *perros de la guerra* win."

Dogs of war. Álvaro had told me that was an inside joke among the foot soldiers. They were *los criados*. The peons, the servants. They called Hector and El Tiburón *perros de la guerra* as an insult.

"No, *'mano*, I'm one of the big dogs now. *Los criados* do what I say." Mario shined the flashlight past Álvaro to the back of the cave where I was hiding behind cartons of foodstuff. "*¿Dónde está tu familia?*"

"My family is safe. Far away from here."

"We'll find them. El Tiburón had Maria Luisa killed. He will kill your wife and boy, too."

"*Los perros de guerra* take no prisoners," said Álvaro. "And neither do we."

He dropped to the floor, and I stepped out from behind the boxes. I couldn't see Mario because the flashlight was pointed in my direction, blinding me. I aimed for the flashlight and fired the pistol. I was well acquainted with this gun. Álvaro and I had prepared for scenarios such as this.

Adjusting my aim, I immediately fired a few inches higher, hoping I had scored a torso and a head shot.

I saw the flashlight fall and heard the unmistakable sound of a body hitting the ground. Keeping the gun aimed in that direction, I crept forward. Álvaro hit the switch on the generator and light flooded the cave.

Mario had a fatal chest wound but the coup de grâce was the center headshot. It had entered where his nose was and obliterated his face. I said a prayer of thanks to my father who had taken me hunting every fall and taught me not to be afraid of guns.

And then I threw up.

I hadn't liked hunting as a child, but I went because it was the only time my father paid attention to me. We'd build a fire and camp out in the woods. During the day, we would sit in a tree stand. I was the lookout, scouting for bucks.

I never killed a deer when I hunted with my father. But I did kill a coyote once with Álvaro.

Álvaro and I practiced shooting regularly. We set up targets on our property; Álvaro had to be certain I was comfortable with both our handgun and rifle. I was actually a better shot than him, much to his amusement. Whenever I was on a roll and hitting the targets consistently, he'd pat me on the behind and say, "Good shooting today, Pancho Villa."

One late afternoon, we were packing up our targets and guns when we heard a low growl and rustling in the brush. Álvaro had already put his rifle away, but I had the Glock in my hand. A large coyote charged out of the shrubs. I aimed and fired, killing the coyote in mid-air, less than a foot away from Álvaro.

Álvaro stumbled back and the coyote fell on top of him. He was trembling as he rolled its body off him. Bloodied from the wound on the coyote and his face white with fear, he clung to me for a moment. "Good shooting, Pancho, good shooting."

I looked down at Mario's lifeless body. He had threatened me and my son. He intended to take my husband captive and turn him over to El Tiburón, who would certainly execute him.

I did what I had to do. But I was sick about it. And my husband hadn't even said thank you.

CHAPTER THIRTY-SEVEN

The sun was just beginning to crest the mountains, so Álvaro turned off the generator. I sat on the blankets where I had slept and wept. My nerves were shot.

"Don't feel sorry for Mario," commanded Álvaro. "If you hadn't killed him, neither you nor I would be alive right now." He made coffee in an aluminum pot on a kerosene camp stove and handed me a cup. The warmth of the tin cup soothed my jangled nerves.

"How many people did you kill when you worked for El Tiburón?" I asked my husband.

"Even though I was the numbers guy, I was often caught up in turf wars with rival gangs. I've killed more than I want to remember." He sighed. "I had hoped and prayed that was all behind me."

We sat side by side on the ledge outside the cave, watching as the golden light crept over the city, eradicating the shadows, and illuminating the streets block by block.

We both knew this was the last view we would ever have of our beloved Taxco.

"What happened? Did Mario come to the house?"

"No, but I saw him drive by the house several times yesterday morning. He had two tough-looking thugs in the back of his pickup truck.

"I wanted to get you and Azul out of the country as quickly as possible, so I staged the house to look like I had been injured and kidnapped. I thought you would follow the plan and take him to Canada. Then I would meet you in a few days." His voice is still hard and angry.

I tentatively touched Álvaro's hand. He pulled it away from me.

"I'm so sorry. . .I didn't know."

"You put our son in great danger. You should have followed the plan. That you didn't is unforgivable."

"You were right. I should never have let Zuzu go alone."

"I am thankful he is safe with your mother." He pulled a blanket around himself to ward off the morning chill. "We can't risk flying now that El Tiburón knows I'm alive. There are still the two thugs who were with Mario that we might have to contend with."

"Couldn't we fly out of another airport? Monterey or Mérida, perhaps?"

He shook his head. "It's too dangerous."

"Which is safer, bus or car?"

When Álvaro looked at me, I could see the uncertainty in his eyes. "*No sé*. I don't know. Probably neither. It's a gamble either way."

"Should we travel alone or together? Maybe one of us go by car and one of us by bus?"

He didn't answer me. There was no right answer. He just shrugged.

Álvaro searched Mario's body. His keys and wallet went into our escape bag. Álvaro smashed his phone with a rock. He removed the sim card from his own phone and smashed it, too.

We stacked our supplies out of sight in the rear of the cave and then rolled Mario's body out of the entrance. It tumbled down the steep slope and was quickly out of sight. Álvaro and I hiked down the mountain in silence.

I was relieved to find our car was still hidden behind the scrub brush where I had left it. While Álvaro checked it thoroughly for tracking devices, I examined the tires and opened the hood. Thankfully, Mario had not incapacitated the car in any way.

CHAPTER THIRTY-EIGHT

We gassed up for the trip in Cuernavaca and filled two gas cans so we wouldn't have to stop for gas again until we were in the United States. I purchased a cooler and packed it with water, juice, tamales, and cooked rice and beans. The fewer times we stopped and interacted with people, the greater the chance we would get out of Mexico alive.

Our plan was to get to the coast, traveling through small towns and avoiding major highways. We would then head north, and cross into the United States at Matamoros. If we drove all day and most of the night, we could reach the border before dawn.

In Tampico, Álvaro purchased a new phone and called my mother. "Your mother is expecting us to be on a flight today," he explained to me. "She will be worried if we don't show up tonight and she might call the authorities. We cannot risk anyone searching for us."

My mother answered the phone on the first ring. "Señora Cassidy, we are experiencing a slight delay. It will be two or three days before we reach Atlanta."

My mother's voice sounded different than I remembered. She was always annoyed when she spoke to me as a child. Now, there was a relaxed softness in her voice.

"Is everything all right, Álvaro? Are you and Eve safe?"

"*Si, Señora*, we are fine. Do not worry. We will see you in a few days."

"Álvaro, wait! Please. Please let me speak to Eve." For a moment her voice hardened. "How do I know you are not a kidnapper? How do I know she is alive? Why won't you let me speak to her?"

I was listening to the entire conversation on speaker. I shook my head and whispered, "No."

"*Señora*, I'm so sorry, but Eva does not want to speak to you. Not yet. May I please speak with my son now?"

My mother sighed. I could hear the sadness in her voice. "Of course. Danny, tell Azul his father is on the phone."

I heard running footsteps. My boy. My Zuzu.

"PAPI! MAMI!" he shouted. "We built a fort in the backyard and me an' Grandpa slept out there last night! I named all the constellations for Grandpa."

I broke down in tears when I heard his voice. "Hi, *piquito*," I said, fully aware that my mother was listening. "Mami loves you so much! I'm so glad you are having fun with your grandmother and grandfather."

Álvaro joined in. "We'll be there soon, *hijo*. No *te preocupas.*"

"Papi, I'm not worried. Grandma and Grandpa are so much fun!"

"*Te veremos pronto, mi amorcito.* We will see you soon, darling."

I heard a voice in the background. "Hey, buddy, let me speak to your mom and dad."

Oh, great, I thought, now my mother's husband, an absolute stranger, is going to butt in. She must have filled his head with all kinds of horrible things about me.

"This is Danny Chan, your mother's, uh, husband. Listen, I'm a detective with the Atlanta PD. If I can help you in any way, if you need anything, just give us a call, Ok? I'm going to text my mobile number to you. Any time of day or night, if you need anything, let me know."

Well, that was unexpected. He sounded nice.

Before we ended the call, I heard my mother say, "Eve, I love you."

We ate a quick lunch at a park by the river and then continued our journey north. It was my turn to drive, and I couldn't help but go over the speed limit. I wanted to sleep in a nice comfortable bed tonight in Brownsville, Texas.

We drove in silence. Once I reached out to touch Álvaro's knee and he shifted in his seat away from me. There was a hardness in his voice when he spoke. "You are being cruel. Why won't you speak to your mother?"

"I'm afraid."

"Afraid? Of What?"

"That I will like her."

CHAPTER THIRTY-NINE

"She seems likeable to me. Why are you afraid to like her?"

I spoke softly, barely above a whisper. I didn't want to admit this to myself, much less to my husband.

"Because, if I like her, it means I was wrong all those years ago to run away. It means I caused all this pain to so many people out of immaturity and selfishness."

Álvaro did not defend me. "You need to look very carefully at your motivation for your actions when you were seventeen and your actions now. You are very selfish, Eva."

His cruel words sliced into my heart like a machete. I could not fathom his anger. We rarely disagreed and never fought. This was out of character.

"I've not told you much about my family. My mother died when I was eight years old. My father turned me and Maria Luisa out on the streets the day she was killed."

"Oh, *cariño*, I'm so sorry."

I'm not sure he heard me. When he spoke, his voice was low. "I know exactly how Zuzu felt walking onto that airplane alone. He was terrified. Desolate. You abandoned our son, Eva!"

He reached into the backseat for his duffle bag. He opened it and removed a book.

I almost swerved off the road. It was a Spanish copy of one of my mother's books. "Where did you get that?"

"When I was in Mexico City last year visiting one of our distributors, I saw some of your mother's books in a bookstore window. I bought this one. I was curious about your family."

I didn't know what to say. It felt like a slight betrayal. Why hadn't he told me? What else was he keeping from me?

"The stories you tell about your mother and the kind of person she was, do not align with what I've read in this book. You told me she was selfish and neglectful. You said she was angry all the time. That's not the person who wrote this book."

I did not tell Álvaro that I, too, had read the book.

CHAPTER FORTY

Shortly after Azul turned five, I started having panic attacks. I had become friendly with a therapist who was the mother of one of Azul's schoolmates. We would meet occasionally for coffee or lunch. One day I mentioned how I was feeling. Isabella suggested we have a few informal sessions.

It wasn't long before she suggested that my anxiety could be about the fear that I would have the same kind of relationship with my child that I had with my mother.

I was shocked when she handed me a book and recommended that I read it. *El Hambre De Amor. Love Hungry.* By Caroline Cassidy.

I was reluctant to read it at first. What did this woman have to say that could possibly be pertinent to me? And when I read it, I was angry. *Why wasn't my mother this kind and insightful when she was raising me?*

All the thoughts and feelings about my mother that I had kept submerged for decades, came flooding back. Suddenly I was seventeen again. "She doesn't love me." "She doesn't understand me." "She is so stupid." "She is so old fashioned."

"Are you certain that she did not love you?" asked Isabella. It took a while for me to admit that she probably did love me in a very distorted way. Just not the way that I needed.

Her next question was, "How did you react to the belief that your mother didn't love you?"

My entire existence was shaped by the belief she did not love me. I ran away from home and had no contact with her for decades.

Isabella asked the next question very gently. "Eva, what is the price you have paid for the belief that your mother didn't love you?"

Oh my god.

How long have we got, Isabella, because that list is so damn long.

CHAPTER FORTY-ONE

I couldn't finish the session that day. I left Isabella's office crying.

The question reverberated in my head, though. "What had these thoughts cost me?"

The price I paid was devastatingly clear. That belief had orphaned me. That belief had caused my parents to have to try to get through every day of their lives not knowing if their child was dead or alive.

It was too much to bear and I descended into a black hole of depression. I stopped seeing Isabella. I avoided her during school drop offs and pickups.

I tried to distract myself from the shadows nibbling at the edge of my sanity. I started taking yoga. I spent more hours at the studio mentoring the apprentices. I took up *knitting*, for goodness' sake.

But I couldn't escape the question. Knit one, purl two… *what have those thoughts cost you?*

One day, Isabella knocked on our door. I didn't answer. She knocked again. That damn woman stood there knocking for fifteen minutes until I answered the door. She held out a bag of my favorite cream filled pastries from *La Pastelería*. I collapsed into her arms, sobbing.

I started therapy with her again. This time I told her the truth—my mother is Caroline Cassidy. I have not had contact with her for over twenty years. Isabella never judged me, nor did she judge my mother. "Sometimes good people act in ways that are not so good."

"I can't help but feel that I am a horrible person for running away. I ruined my mother's life. What if I ruin my son's life, too?"

"Eva, you are a good person. I notice how you parent Azul. I see the type of relationship you and Álvaro have—it is loving and healthy. I know some of your employees and they speak very highly of you and Álvaro."

Isabella picked up my mother's book. "This is not a person whose life was ruined. This is a person who overcame many adverse circumstances and created a good life for herself."

She opened the book to the first page. "She talks about her regret for failing someone she loved very much. Listen.

"This book is dedicated to Evie. You may never know how much I love you. I'm sorry I failed to show up for you. If I ever get another chance, I promise I will do better now that I know better."

She turned to another marked page.

"I realized I have the power to create my own destiny and everything that happens to me actually happens for me—to further me on the path to enlightenment." Isabella looked up from the book. "That doesn't sound like a woman who felt the victim of circumstances. It is actually a very healthy philosophy to believe that things show up in our lives to assist us in becoming the people we are supposed to be."

Isabella put down the book and took my hands in hers. "What if, the person you became because you ran away, and because you met Álvaro and married him, is the person you were supposed to become all along? What if that was the path to your best life?

"All it takes is a shift in perspective. You didn't make a mistake. You followed your soul's calling to your authentic self."

CHAPTER FORTY-TWO

For the last nine months I have been in therapy with Isabella. I have willingly put my life under the microscope. I scrutinized the beliefs and actions of the cheerleader and Homecoming Queen who left home so long ago.

Isabella helped me see the shift I had made from believing my mother had ruined my life to believing that it was inevitable that I would ruin my child's life. "Neither belief is true, Eva.

"When we become parents ourselves, we gain a whole new perspective on the people who parented us. The narrow one-sided view we had as children expands and the whole picture becomes clear. The rules and restrictions that once seemed draconian and unreasonable, we now understand were guidelines that provided a framework in which our maturing emotions could safely operate and explore."

I was thankful for Isabella's gentle approach. She didn't push or prod me. She provided the container in which my soul could find the answers for itself.

"You can forgive yourself. If you don't love yourself first, you can't love anyone else."

That was another line from my mother's book. When had she become so wise? Is it possible that my leaving also propelled my mother into her own search for significance? Was that the catalyst for her own transformative journey?

Isabella smiled. "What should be, will be, Eva."

Another quote from my mother. Damn.

CHAPTER FORTY-THREE

W e crossed the border at Brownsville at 1:00 a.m. with Canadian passports and identification. By 2:00 a.m. we were fast asleep in a noisy motel by the highway. The constant roar of cars and trucks didn't keep us awake. We were exhausted from the drama of the past two days. And excited—Atlanta, and Azul, were only 20 hours away.

Our plan was to pick up Azul and drive to Canada soon after. The house on Vancouver Island was ready—I had taken one trip three years ago to furnish it and purchase household goods. A management company looked after it in our absence.

I heard Álvaro stirring before daylight.

"I can't sleep. I am anxious to see Zuzu."

"Me, too." I washed my face and dressed. "Let's go get our son."

The flats of Texas were as colorless and lifeless as our moods. We went for hours without speaking, Álvaro only making a comment or asking a question when necessary.

Houston. New Orleans. Birmingham. We were on the home stretch by 7:00 p.m. Only an hour and a half to my mother's house in Georgia.

"Are you nervous to see your mother again?"

"I'm not sure if nervous is the right word. More like terrified.

"I've worked with Isabella for almost a year to put the last two decades in perspective. I've worked on forgiving myself and my mother. What if she hasn't forgiven me? What if we fall right back into the old relationship patterns of misunderstandings and criticism? What if I...."

Álvaro interrupted me. "Stop with the negative thinking. What if your mother welcomes you with open arms? What if she does not blame you or shame you?"

I looked side-eyed at Álvaro. "You don't know my mother."

"And neither do you." His voice was steely. "Not anymore. Give her the grace you want her to give you."

After twenty-six years of marriage, was my husband taking my mother's side against me?

CHAPTER FORTY-FOUR

The door to my mother's stone cottage opened as soon as we parked in the gravel driveway. Azul flew down the steps, we jumped out of the car, and the three of us held each other tight. Out of the corner of my eye, I saw my mother observing us.

She had changed. A little heavier, a lot grayer. But it was her countenance that was the most strikingly different. I can best describe it as "radiant." That's not what I expected.

She and Danny gave us space to reconnect with Azul and then he was pulling us up the steps to the house.

I paused before my mother while Azul dragged Álvaro through the door.

"Hello, Caroline."

She took my face in her hands. "My goodness, Eve, you are so beautiful. Breathtaking."

I was not expecting the gentleness with which she spoke. "My darling Eve. My darling girl." She gathered me into her arms, and I dissolved into a puddle of tears on her front porch.

CHAPTER FORTY-FIVE

She held me while I sobbed. This is what I had needed so long ago: understanding, acceptance, and love. If only my mother had. . .

No. I made a choice not to go there. No more "if only." Isabella had counseled me to stay with "what is," in the present. "The more you dwell on the past, the more you are trapped in those negative emotions and thoughts."

My mother broke our embrace and held me at arm's length. "Forgive me, Eve, for failing you so often and so deeply." She brushed the tears from my cheeks and then wiped away her own. "It's late and I know you are exhausted. Let's go inside and eat dinner. There will be time to talk later."

My mother's house was a two-story stone cottage on the edge of the campus of Peachtree College in Decatur, Georgia. The living room was simply furnished with a denim-covered sofa and several comfortable armchairs in retro prints. The sound of laughter and lively chatter drew me into the kitchen.

I heard Azul tell Álvaro, "Papi, I helped Grandpa Dan make the pop pie!"

Danny was dishing up chicken pot pie around the kitchen table. We were about to dig in when Azul sighed, looked around the table, and said, "All my favorite people are here."

"Amen, buddy," said Danny. "Mine, too." He took my mother's hand in his and kissed it. Then he raised his wineglass in a toast and said, "To love. It is not an easy path, and it takes a lot of faith to endure the journey. But in the end, love wins."

We all echoed, "Amen."

"*Dios mio*, this is delicious!" I exclaimed after my first bite. When did my mother learn to cook like this? I remembered take-out and fast-food meals for most of my childhood.

"Thank you. Marci is teaching me how to cook," Danny said proudly. He pointed to my mother and said in a fake whisper, "Your mother isn't the greatest cook."

He regaled us with the story of the first meal she cooked for him. She had made lasagna but didn't realize the noodles had to be boiled prior to assembling the casserole. Nor did she realize the meat needed to be cooked before adding the sauce.

I watched my mother to see how she would react to the story. During my childhood, any mention by my father of a failure on her part was met with a stony glare and days of petulant silence.

My mother was laughing so hard she had tears in her eyes. "It was awful! I did not have a clue how to make lasagna. It was just one big ugly blob! I don't know why I didn't ask Marci to make it and pass it off as my own."

I remembered Marci King, my mother's best friend from childhood. "Marci is a cook?"

"Much more than that. Marci is the owner of the most popular restaurant in Decatur. We'll have breakfast there tomorrow. Her biscuits are heavenly."

After dinner, my mother led me into the living room while Danny and Álvaro did the dishes. Azul settled himself into my lap and put his thumb in his mouth. He hadn't sucked his thumb since infancy. The events of the last few days had taken a toll on my boy.

"Mom, how is dad?"

My mother's countenance fell. "Honey, I'm so sorry. Your dad died in 2016."

I checked in, as Isabella had taught me, to see how that made me feel. Sad. Regretful. He died without knowing I was ok. "How?"

"He had a heart attack. It was. . .he didn't survive it."

"Were you still married?"

"No, we divorced a few years after. . ." Her voice trailed off. I knew what she meant.

"Was he still a minister when he died?"

"He was. He had remarried." My mother paused. "We weren't friends. I tried to maintain some type of relationship with him, but he refused. He was very angry with me for leaving."

"Where is his. . .where is he buried?" I needed closure with my dad.

"In the church graveyard." She touched my hand. "We can go there together if you'd like. I have a few things I'd like to say to him, too."

Azul had fallen asleep in my lap.

"It's after midnight. Let's get this boy into bed. We made a little room for him in the loft."

My mother pointed upstairs. "You can stay here tonight. Danny and I will go to his place and sleep. We'll come over around 11:00 tomorrow morning and go to Marci's."

"We can get a hotel. We don't want to inconvenience you."

My mother smiled. "You can get a hotel tomorrow if you'd like. Danny and I are packed, and his house is not far from here."

"Danny seems really nice, Mom."

"He is. You won't believe how we met, but that's a very long story for another day."

My heart was divided. I had twenty-six years of stories to catch up with. But we also needed to leave Atlanta for Canada as soon as possible. El Tiburón's cartel was headquartered in Atlanta. According to Mario, there was a three-million-dollar bounty they would be looking to collect.

We didn't know how much information about us Mario had communicated to El Tiburón. What we did know is that El Tiburón was still actively looking for us.

Álvaro carried Azul up the stairs and put him to bed in the loft. We tucked him in with his teddy bear and both bent down to kiss him. He smiled in his sleep and burrowed under his blanket. All was right in his little world again. I would move heaven and earth to keep it that way.

CHAPTER FORTY-SIX

My mother had turned down the bed and laid fresh towels on the dresser. Two beautifully scented candles were lit, one in the bedroom and one in the bathroom. While the downstairs rooms were simple, she had spared no expense in her suite. The bathroom was as luxurious as a five-star hotel. A soaking tub stood in front of a large window. Outside the window was a tall oak tree, hung with twinkling lights. It reminded me of that tree so long ago in Torreon where I had fallen in love with Álvaro and Mexico.

I was instantly envious of her closet. It was huge, as big as her bath and bedroom combined. A chair and a small table sat in the center of the room. Floor to ceiling shelves lined each wall, with built in dressers and hanging space placed strategically. An entire wall of shelving displayed rocks and crystals, candles, books, small statues, and a few vignettes that looked like altars. I recognized a few photographs of me as a child and teenager, set in a semi-circle around a large pink stone heart. There were smaller purple and black stones scattered around the pink stone. What looked like a page from a diary in mother's handwriting was propped against one of my photographs. The ink was smudged from what were surely my mother's tears.

"My darling Victoria Eve, where are you? I am sick with worry and my heart is shattered. I pray your guardian angels will protect you until your path leads you home.

It was dated December 25, 1997.

I recognized a folded lavender piece of paper underneath the pink rock.

I unfolded it and read the last communication I had with my parents.

"John and Caroline, I don't know why you two ever thought having a child was a good idea. Was it so you could have a little show pony for your congregation? You ignore me until it is time for us to act like a perfect family in public.

Did you even know I won Homecoming Queen? No, because you were both too busy with God and your damn books to even care about coming to the game. Or, to ask me about it afterward.

Don't blame anyone else for my leaving, not Jett, not me. This is all on you."

CHAPTER FORTY-SEVEN

My stomach lurched. As a parent myself now, I can imagine the grief those words caused my mother and father. The imprint of heartache on their souls would last forever.

I had a dreadful thought. Is this why my father died? Had I literally broken his heart?

Álvaro walked into the closet, his hair wet from the shower, smelling of vetiver and lemongrass.

When he saw my face, he asked, "What's wrong?"

I put the note behind my back. There was no reason to give him additional ammunition against me.

"Just dealing with all this. And finding out that my father is dead."

He noticed the photographs of me on the shelf. He picked up the card my mother had written. "May I?"

His formality is irritating.

He read the note my mother had written so long ago when she realized her only daughter had left home for good. "Your mother is a remarkable woman."

"She hasn't always been so wonderful."

"So you say. But I saw much grace tonight. No one was making accusations or shifting blame."

I've had it with his bias. "Are you going to stay angry with me?"

"You endangered my son. I'm not ready to forgive you."

He's right. I did endanger Azul. I see that now. I need Álvaro's forgiveness before I can forgive myself.

When he first met me, he could have written me off as a teenage troublemaker or spoiled little rich girl. In truth, I was both. Instead, he chose to look past appearances and first impressions, scrying deep into my heart to see the real me.

Now, I need him to look past the fact that I betrayed his trust. I am drowning in shame. I am terrified that I have become everything I hated about my mother.

She, on the other hand, seems to have morphed into a cross between Princess Diana and Oprah.

He didn't answer my question. "Let's get a good night sleep and tomorrow we can decide when we leave for Canada." Álvaro turned out the light and got into bed. He lay with his back to me, close to the edge on his side. I touched his shoulder, rubbing his back and arm. He stiffened and moved closer to the edge of the bed.

I tossed and turned for several hours. I wasn't feeling well so I got up and looked in my mother's medicine cabinet. The crunch of footsteps outside on the gravel drive startled me. I woke Álvaro. "Someone's outside with a flashlight."

We looked out the window and saw two men casting light on our car, examining the license plate, and looking in the windows. Álvaro immediately called Danny.

"Make certain the front and back doors are locked. I'll call 911. Do you know how to use a gun?" Álvaro assured him he did. Danny gave him the gun safe code. "Be careful, son. I'll be right there."

Álvaro moved Azul to my mother's bed. We closed the door and went downstairs. A police officer was knocking on the door within minutes.

One officer waited outside while the other came inside with us. "Detective Chan asked us to wait until he got here. The intruders are gone. They fled through the woods when they saw us approaching."

I made coffee and took a cup to the officer outside. We sat in the living room with the officer until Danny and my mother arrived.

"I'm George Wilson. I picked up your son from the airport and brought him here. He sure is a cute little fellow."

"Thank you, Officer Wilson, for delivering him safely."

My mother burst through the door and came to my side. "Are you all ok?"

"Yes, we are. I had a headache and got up to look for medicine. That's when I noticed someone outside trying to break into our car."

"Danny will be in shortly. The officer is about to dust the car for prints."

Álvaro quickly stepped outside. "Danny, can I talk to you?"

They conferred on the front porch for several minutes, their voices never rising above a whisper.

My mother and I looked at each other in confusion.

Danny and Álvaro came inside. "George, thank you for responding so quickly. If you'll make a report about trespassing and suspicious activity, we will leave it at that. No need to dust the car for prints—whoever was out there never touched it."

I looked at Álvaro. We had both seen and heard one of the men try each door handle. Álvaro slightly shook his head, indicating I should remain quiet.

Danny asked the two officers to remain until he could get some off-duty men here for round-the-clock protection. My mother called Marci and asked her to send over breakfast and pastries for all of us. We were going to stay put for the day and plan our next move.

The four of us gathered around the kitchen table drinking coffee.

"What were you two whispering about on the porch? And why didn't they dust the car for prints?"

"It's a long and complicated story," Álvaro began.

"I've got time," I said. "And I'll bet your story isn't half as complicated as this one." I circled my finger in the air, indicating my mother and me.

"You've already lost that bet."

CHAPTER FORTY-EIGHT

"Eva, I have not been entirely truthful with you about why I left Atlanta and what I did for El Tiburón."

I rose from the table and walked over to the bar cart. I picked up a bottle of Bailey's and poured a splash into my coffee. My mother held out her cup for some as well.

I gestured for Álvaro to continue. Two of us could play the silent judging game.

"I was El Tiburón's accountant. And Hector Garcia was skimming off the top. That much is true. But I was also working undercover. I was a DEA agent, reporting on El Tiburón's operation.

"I killed Hector because he discovered my ruse and was going to expose me. Maria Luisa was killed in retaliation."

Danny asked, "Do you know who informed on you? How did Hector find out you were DEA?"

"Mexico is rife with corrupt *federales*. It could have been any number of government officials looking to cash in on that kind of information. I knew I didn't want to end up like Kiki Camarena." Álvaro looked at me. "That's why I didn't want the police to dust the car for prints. When I left Atlanta, I went AWOL from the DEA."

"Who's Kiki Camarena?"

"Enrique Camarena was a DEA agent who was abducted, tortured, and murdered in 1985. He was informed on by a few Mexican politicians working for the Guadalajara Cartel."

My mother spoke up. "Then why go to Mexico to live? Wasn't that more dangerous? Wouldn't it be more likely that you would be recognized there?"

"I was planning to go to Canada, but first had to retrieve some documents and cash from a safe deposit box in Taxco. That's where I was headed when I met Eva."

"You said you were headed to Acapulco."

"I didn't know you. You could have been a plant, an informant. I was wary of everyone at that point. So, yes, that was a misdirection.

"Once I got to know you, I decided it might be better to hide in plain sight, where El Tiburón would least expect to find me."

I wished Álvaro had said, "Once I fell in love with you," but he hadn't.

"What about the DEA?" asked Danny. "Didn't they offer protection?"

"They did, but I didn't know who was compromised and would sell me out. Kiki was offered protection, too, but they still got to him. There was no time to resign. I just disappeared."

Danny continued his thoughts. "I'm more than a little concerned that El Tiburón's men found you so quickly. Have you checked your car for tracking devices?"

"We did when we left Taxco. I didn't find anything."

Danny stood up. "Let's get some flashlights and look a little more thoroughly."

Forty-five minutes later they brought two tiny little buttons into the house and laid them on the table.

"It was well hidden," Danny said. "I would have missed it, too. We had to remove the spare tire to find it. The second one was on our car, the one we left here overnight. They were planning to track all of us."

Danny put his hands on his hips and looked at me. "We need to put you, Azul, and Cal somewhere safe."

"What about you two?"

"We're going after El Tiburón."

CHAPTER FORTY-NINE

M y mother and I shouted at the same time.
"Like hell you are, Danny Chan."

"Have you lost your mind? Absolutely not. We'll be safe in Canada."

Danny and Mom looked at me. "Canada?"

"We still have a few things in our favor," said Álvaro. "We have new identities. Canadian. We bought a house there a few years ago through a shell corporation. Untraceable back to us. We will be safe there.

"We were planning to pick up Azul and head to Canada within the next few days." I put my arm around my mother. "After we got to know each other again."

Mom grinned and smacked me on the cheek with her lips. "And after we kissed and made up?"

I laughed. "Yeah, something like that. There's still so much I want to ask and talk about. For instance, what's with all the crystals and voodoo paraphernalia in your closet?"

Danny comically rolled his eyes. "Don't get your mother started on her magical mystery tour. Seriously, ladies, I appreciate the levity, but you need to pack your bags. We need to move quickly."

There was a knock at the door. Danny approached the door with his gun drawn. It reminded me of the time in El Paso when Álvaro opened the door the same way. All along there were clues that there was more to Álvaro's story than he was telling me. I just hadn't wanted to see it.

Marci entered with bags of food that smelled delicious. She looked at Danny, gun in hand. "What's up, Sheriff? I swear I didn't do it."

She dropped the bags on the table when she saw me and gave me a bear hug. "Evie, oh Evie," is all she said. She pinched my cheeks. "You are the spitting image of your Auntie Marilyn. Beautiful."

She then turned to Álvaro. "And what have we here?" She looked him up and down and then looked at me. "You go, girl," and gave a little cheetah growl. Marci had not changed a bit. She was still my mother's wise-cracking fun-loving best friend, and partner in crime.

"I would love to stay and catch up, but we've got a record houseful at Serendipity this morning." As she was running out the door and down the steps she shouted, "I'll be back tonight, and I'll bring dinner!"

Danny laughed. "Hello and goodbye, Hurricane Marci. Let's eat."

I was thankful Azul was sleeping in. We had a lot to discuss that I didn't want him to hear. He had been traumatized enough in the last few days. And there was more to come. We were moving to a new country, leaving behind the only life and people he had known for five years.

I knew Danny was right. The only way to keep El Tiburón from coming after us was to eliminate him.

Or was it? I remembered Álvaro's ruse to make it appear he had been kidnapped so that I would head to Canada with Azul.

If El Tiburón believed Álvaro was dead, would he leave me and Azul alone?

"Kiki Camarena's wife—is she still alive?"

Álvaro answered. "Yes, I believe she lives in California with their son."

"What if we fake your death, Álvaro? Wouldn't that end the vendetta against you? He has no reason to come after me and Azul."

"Proving my death would be impossible. The only proof El Tiburón accepts as proof of the death of his enemies is their heads. Nothing else would work."

"Anyone ever heard of Photoshop? We could doctor up photos and. . ."

"I mean my actual head. Not a photograph. No, the only way to be certain we are safe from El Tiburón is to remove him from the equation. Permanently."

CHAPTER FIFTY

The plan to leave for Canada was vetoed by Álvaro. "I will not let Azul out of my sight," he said sternly. I saw a look pass between my mother and Danny. The tension between me and my husband was apparent.

I turned to Danny for advice. "Is it safe for us to stay in Atlanta?"

He thought for a moment. "You have new identities, ones you've not used before, correct?"

"Yes. We just used them for the first time to cross the border."

He conferred with Álvaro. "What if we put them in a safe house with 24-hour protection? It's simplistic but it could work. Use your new identity to rent an Airbnb with enough rooms to house 4 security guards, plus the five of us.

"I'll arrange security with a private firm a buddy of mine owns. Cal, go upstairs with Álvaro and book an Airbnb on my precinct network.

He looked at Álvaro. "You have credit cards in your new names?"

Álvaro nodded. "Yes."

While Álvaro and my mother booked an Airbnb, I packed our belongings. Azul stirred and stretched. "Guess what, Zuzu? We are going on a little vacation with Grandpa and Grandma!"

Azul looked panicked. "Are you and Papi coming, too? Don't leave me again, Mami."

I gathered my son in my arms. "I won't leave you, *piquito*." I felt a shudder of fear in his little body and then he relaxed.

What had I done? To what extent have I damaged my marriage and my son? I took note of Azul's fear and thought about Álvaro. He had never shared much about his parents or his childhood. I was so wrapped up in my own family drama that I never thought to delve into his. Perhaps if I had not been so self-absorbed I would have a better understanding of my husband's feelings.

Has my entire life has been a series of rash actions with devastating consequences on those closest to me—my parents, my husband, and my son? I desperately wished I could talk things over with Isabella. Immersed in the emotion of my reunion with my mother, I felt the progress I had made in therapy was slowly eroding.

A bizarre thought popped into my head. My mother and I were about to be cooped up together for the next few weeks.

Is it possible she could help me navigate this crisis with Álvaro?

I began planning my approach to ask my mother for help. And then I realized I had not yet said the words that must be said first, before anything else—"Mom, I'm sorry. Please forgive me."

CHAPTER FIFTY-ONE

My mother came downstairs with a small suitcase. "You know we'll be gone for at least a few weeks, right?" I asked, nodding to her small bag.

She smiled. "I've got some tee shirts and a couple pair of leggings. And a pair of jeans."

Who was this woman? The Caroline Cassidy I knew was always perfectly and immaculately dressed "for success" and would never leave the house without a full complement of makeup and coiffed hair. Maybe without a congregation to cater to or impress she was less concerned about what other people thought about her.

I put her suitcase in my car and asked her to ride with me. Álvaro had no problem when I asked him and Azul to ride with Danny.

Danny gave me the address of the Airbnb. "You take the lead, and we'll follow. Don't run yellow lights and don't pull out into traffic and lose us. It's safer if we stay together."

A woman I didn't know pulled into the driveway just before we left. Danny introduced me to his partner, a detective named Biz. When Azul saw her, he ran to her. "Bizzy!"

The woman scooped up Azul and gave him a kiss. She whispered something in his ear, and he burst out laughing. It was obvious my son had charmed all the grown-ups in my mother's world.

"I'll be following you guys to make sure you don't have anyone tagging along. The narcotics squad has had eyes on El Tiburón since this morning but there may be some unknowns out there."

We left my mother's house caravan-style. Danny followed me closely, keeping less than a car's length between us. Biz stayed much further back from Danny's car, looking for any suspicious vehicles tailing us.

I took a deep breath. "Mom, I want to apologize to you." She laid her hand on my shoulder and left it there. It was a comfortable feeling, especially since Álvaro and I had not had much physical contact lately.

Tears ran down my cheeks. "I am so sorry for leaving the way I did and never letting you know I was okay."

My mother smiled. "I knew you were safe, Evie. I didn't know where you were, but I knew deep in my heart that if something bad had happened to you, I would have felt it. Remember the time you jumped off the bunk bed and knocked your front teeth out when you were three?"

I nodded. I had been staying with my Aunt Marilyn while my parents went to a church conference for a few days.

"Coming back from the conference, I had a horrible feeling come over me. I knew something had happened to you. Your father said I was crazy, but I knew. And sure enough, when we got to Marilyn's house she was holding an ice bag to your face.

"It's I that should apologize to you, love. You were just a child, and I was not there for you. I was too wrapped up in my own pain and my own ambition to notice what you were going through. I never blamed you for leaving. I blamed myself."

My mother's words surprised me. I thought she would have a hard time forgiving me for what I had done. Or was I projecting my own guilt? Wasn't it true that I was having a hard time forgiving myself?

We were coming up to a large intersection, Ponce de Leon and Briarcliff. I was so engrossed in my thoughts that I didn't notice the light turned yellow just before I went through the intersection.

The sound of metal crashing into metal woke me from my reverie. I looked in my rear-view mirror as my mother turned around in her seat. What we saw was terrifying. Two SUVs had broadsided Danny's car in the intersection. The push-guards on the front of the SUVs had bashed in both sides of the car. We could see Danny and Álvaro struggling to get the doors open but they were jammed.

Dear God, Danny, Álvaro, and Azul were sitting ducks. They would be slaughtered by El Tiburón's men.

I slammed on my brakes. The car behind me laid on their horn. Traffic was heavy and moving slow. I desperately looked for a way to turn around, but the street was packed. I had to keep moving ahead and try to find a side street to double back to my family.

"We've got to help them! I'm looking for a side street to turn around!"

My phone rang and my mother answered it. "Where are you?" shouted Danny.

My mother and I were hysterical. "Is Azul OK? Are you OK? Are they shooting at you?"

My mother put the phone on speaker. I could hear sirens and shouting. "Eve! Whatever you do, don't stop! They hit us to disable our car, but they didn't stop. They are coming after you. Do you see them?"

"Yes!" I could see the black SUVs weaving through traffic, hitting slower-moving cars. As they pushed the cars out of the way, they left a tangled mess of snarled traffic in their wake.

"Can you outrun them?"

"No!" I sobbed. "There's too much traffic ahead of us!"

"Try to make it to the freeway and then drive like a bat out of hell. Every available unit is on the way."

I heard Álvaro softly praying in Spanish for our protection.

We had driven far enough ahead that I could no longer see Danny's car in the rearview mirror. The two SUVs were less than a car length behind us. And then, one swerved in front of us and had us blocked in from the front and side.

Three armed men appeared at my mother's door and motioned for her to open it. When she didn't, one of the men smashed in the window with a crowbar and unlocked the door. They pulled my mother out. They reached in and grabbed me, hauling me over the console and broken glass. They man-handled us into the back of the SUV. As I was shoved into the car, I looked to see if anyone was coming to help us. I could see Biz, about thirty yards back, running at full speed. There was no way she would reach us in time.

I saw the horrified looks of drivers and passengers in the cars surrounding us. No one came to our assistance. I can't blame them. The men who took us were heavily armed.

My mother is not a young woman, but she fought and kicked like a ninja. The thug in the backseat with us took one hand and wrapped it around her neck, squeezing until she was gasping for breath. I clawed the door trying to grasp the door handle, but it wouldn't budge. Neither would the window. The child-locks must have been activated on the backseat doors and windows.

Screaming at the top of my lungs, I reached my arms around the front seat to grab the neck of the driver. The cold steel of a gun barrel against my forehead stopped me.

The man in the backseat with us was a big as a gorilla. He zip-tied our hands and feet and then put duct tape over our mouths.

"You ladies need to calm the fuck down."

CHAPTER FIFTY-TWO

After we were zip-tied and duct taped, a cloth bag was put over our heads. The last glimpse I had of my mother surprised me. She was not frightened. Her eyes were snapping with anger and her jaw set with steely determination. She placed her zip-tied hands on my lap and entwined her fingers around mine.

She laid her head on my shoulder, and I heard her humming a familiar tune. *Rock-a-by baby in the treetops, when the wind blows the cradle will rock.* My mother had changed the words to the nursery rhyme when she sang it to me as a baby. *When the bough breaks the baby will fly, up to the moon and stars in the sky.*

She squeezed my hand. In my mind, I flashed back to my seventeen-year-old self lying on a bus station bathroom floor, having a miscarriage. I remembered how lonely and scared I was, and how I had cried for my mother.

I squeezed back. I realized how much it means to have someone you love by your side when things go wrong.

I was getting sick from the twists and turns in the road. It was hot underneath the bag over my head and sweat was pouring down my face. I yanked the bag off my head and ripped the duct tape off my mouth. It hurt like hell. At least I wouldn't have to shave my upper lip for a while.

I held the bag out in front of me and threw up into it. The man in the front seat turned around and pointed the gun at me again. The gorilla beside my mother pushed the man's arm away. He removed the bag from my mother's head. "Y'all be good now," he said sternly.

My mother carefully removed the tape from her mouth. She lifted her zipped hands to my face and wiped the sweat that was stinging my eyes. Holding up her hands she turned to the man beside her, "Is this totally necessary?"

He produced a switchblade and cut the restraints.

"What's your name, Gorilla?"

The man didn't laugh but he cracked a smile. "You can call me Naja."

As the mother of a child obsessed with reptiles, I knew that a "naja" was a type of cobra.

"Do we have much further to go? I have to pee, and my old bladder will flood this back seat if I have to."

"*¡Carajo!*" Naja held up the roll of duct tape and waved it in front of my mother as a threat. "We're almost there. Hold it."

What the hell was going on with my mother? Was she intentionally trying to irritate our captors?

We were in an industrial park that looked deserted. Abandoned buildings with broken windows and doors hanging off the hinges lined both sides of the one-way street. We pulled into a parking lot in front of a rusted metal warehouse with grimy windows painted black on the inside. There were two armed men standing guard beside a double metal door that retracted like a garage door. The SUV drove into the building.

Naja clipped the zip ties on our legs. "I wouldn't try running if I were you. Or yelling. There is no one around to hear you and we will shoot you in the legs if you run. It would be a shame to shoot you," he shrugged, "but *ni modo.*"

Shooting us would be "no big deal?"

Fear settled into the pit of my stomach and acid rose into my throat. I assumed these men were part of El Tiburón's crew and that we were taken as hostages to punish Álvaro. Mario had said in the cave that El Tiburón killed Álvaro's sister, Maria Luisa. It had not occurred to me until now that we might be raped before we were killed. I threw up again into the muslin bag.

Before the metal door closed, I could hear the roar of trucks and cars. We must be near an expressway. Maybe my mother would have a clue as to where we were.

Then again, what good would that do us? We had no way to contact Álvaro or Danny and let them know our location. If we were going to survive, it would be by our wits. And maybe some of that magic that my mother practiced.

CHAPTER FIFTY-THREE

While the exterior of the warehouse looked abandoned, the interior had been completely renovated. The large open space had a concrete floor and was brightly lit. On both sides of the building was a bank of rooms. We were led to one of the rooms on the left side. Naja lifted a three-inch metal bar, unlocked the door, and gestured for us to enter.

I was surprised when another man followed us into the room, carrying our bags. He unzipped both and dumped the contents onto the king-size bed. He examined everything from my underwear to my face cream. He opened my deodorant and sniffed it. Seriously? Like I'm hiding a master key in my damn deodorant?

He picked up the box that held my mother's tarot cards. I saw a look of fear cross his face. He dropped the box like it was a hot potato. "*¡Brujas!* Witches!"

"That's right," my mother said. "We're witches! And if you're not careful, we are going to cast spells on you. Your children will develop big ugly boils on their faces and your women will be infertile." The man fled in fear.

Naja laughed. "You are a very smart woman, Ms. Cassidy. Señor Salas will be pleased. He is very anxious to meet both of you."

Naja continued. "Unpack your things and make yourselves comfortable. You will be served dinner at 6:00 tonight." He nodded to a bookcase. "There are many things for your amusement. Books, games," he picked up a television remote control, "and Netflix." He handed me a walkie-talkie. "If you need anything, let Chaco know. Although, he may not respond because you scared the *caca* out of him with your witchy talk."

"What the hell is going on? We've been kidnapped; this is not a fucking vacation! I demand to see El Tiburón."

Naja did not react to my mother's outburst. "Señor Salas is not available at the moment. Perhaps tomorrow, or the next day." He left the room without another word. We heard the lock click and the metal barricade slam into place.

"Have you lost your mind?" I yelled at my mother. "Did it not occur to you to use some of your psychological prowess to get us out of this mess? You're making it worse!"

My mother responded calmly. "They are not going to hurt us. I read their body language and facial expressions. Our fate lies in El Tiburón's hands, not these guys. For some reason he is extremely anxious to meet you."

"So, you think we are safe for the moment?"

"Yes. There were several times that Naja could have hurt us, but he didn't. I pushed him to see how he would react, but he restrained himself. They are obviously under orders not to hurt us. Not yet, anyway."

My mother was full of surprises. "I was scared out of my mind in the back seat of the car. How did you keep your cool well enough to administer a psychological test to our captors?"

"Oh, baby, this isn't the worst predicament I've been in. Not too long ago a crazy psychopath framed me for murder and then attempted to kill me to cover up her involvement."

"What? Are you kidding?"

"Not kidding. Wish I was. Except, that's how I met Danny. He is the detective who arrested me and indicted me for murder."

I looked at my mother in amazement. "Who was murdered?"

"Do you want the long version or the short version?"

I looked around the room. "We're not going anywhere any time soon. I want the whole enchilada."

Cool as a cucumber, my mother picked up the two-way radio. "Hey, Chaco, I want two lattes with whipped cream. Breve. And a couple of pastries."

"*Caramba*, you've got cojones."

My mother smiled. "Damn right I do."

CHAPTER FIFTY-FOUR

Fifteen minutes later the door opened. I half expected Naja and his crew, having had enough of my mother's smart-ass outbursts, to mount an assault with guns drawn and shoot us point blank.

Chaco timidly entered the room with two Starbucks cups and a brown paper bag.

I remembered the fights my parents would have when my mother would blurt out some 'squirrelly' thing (my father's word, not mine) he thought irrational or inappropriate. "Caroline, your words and actions are not worthy of a representative of the Lord." In my mother's book, she wrote about her diagnosis of borderline personality disorder. BPD is characterized by impulsiveness, extreme emotions, and acting or doing things without thinking about them first.

My apple did not fall far from my mother's tree. Whenever I was nervous or frightened, I could say and do stupid things. I had talked it over with Isabella. She agreed that it was possible I was a high functioning borderline personality.

Despite my mother's assurances that we were not going to be harmed, I was terrified. So, when Chaco set the food and drinks on the coffee table, I looked him square in the eye, raised my hands like claws, and hissed. The man screamed in terror and backed into an end table, knocking over a lamp.

Naja dashed into the room, reaching for his weapon. He picked up Chaco from the floor and pushed him out the door. "*Traviesas,*" he said, shaking his head. "*Tengan cuidado.*" He sounded stern but I saw a glint of amusement in his eye.

"What did he say?" asked my mother.

"*Traviesa* means 'troublemaker' but in a playful way. When Azul is naughty, I call him *travieso*. *Tengan cuidado* means 'be careful.'"

"If I'm reading him correctly, he didn't sound threatening; more like amused." Blessed Virgen, let my mother be right; she is gambling with our lives.

I couldn't reconcile the incongruency of our situation. We have been kidnapped by a drug cartel that is known for its violence and barbarity. Yet we have just been served lattes and scones by said cartel. It didn't add up.

"I think El Tiburón wants to get a message to Álvaro through you. That's why we were snatched the way we were and why Danny and Álvaro were not harmed and left behind."

"That doesn't make sense."

"It does if the goal is not to kill Álvaro, but to talk with him. For some reason, Mr. Salas doesn't want a confrontation, he wants a meeting. And you are the go-between."

"But why? He put a three million dollar hit on Álvaro. Mario was killed trying to collect it when we killed him."

"Was it a hit, or was Mario's instruction to capture Álvaro and take him to El Tiburón? Maybe Mario went rogue and thought he'd get more if he killed Álvaro. We won't know the truth until Mr. Salas shows up."

I put my hands on my forehead. "I have a raging headache."

"I'll massage your shoulders." She walked over to the bed and picked up a crystal and a small vial. She placed a beautiful dark blue stone in my left hand. When she unscrewed the top of the vial, I smelled peppermint. She rubbed a few drops on her fingertips and began to massage my head and shoulders. Several times she stopped massaging and held her hands above my head. I could feel my head tingling when she did that.

"What are you doing?"

"Reiki. Energy healing."

I was dumbfounded. Magic rocks, fortune telling cards, and enchanted potions. *Dios mio*, my mother really is a witch.

"Did you do any of this stuff when you were married to Dad?"

"After you. . .left, I floundered for a bit, trying to make sense of life. And God."

I didn't interrupt my mother with apologies. We could spend the rest of our lives in a stagnant pool of apologies, or we could move forward in compassion and grace.

She bent forward and kissed the top of my head. I felt a spark, and then an immediate easing of my headache.

"I began to explore what was then known as 'New Age' philosophies. Or 'latter day apostacies' as your father called them. One day I brought home a deck of Tarot cards. He tore them up, burned them in the fireplace and told me never to bring tools of the devil into our home again."

I couldn't help but laugh. "I'm sorry, Mom, but you sounded just like him. I can picture him doing that."

"When I left, he told me I was the devil incarnate."

"I think Álvaro believes I'm a devil, too. He is really angry with me for sending Azul alone on the airplane to Atlanta."

"I'm not worried about you and Álvaro, honey. The energy between you two is strong." She paused for a moment like she was listening to something. I turned to look at her. She had her eyes closed. "He is not reacting to what you did. He's reacting to a past situation, something with his own parents." She opened her eyes and saw me staring at her. "Do you think I'm crazy?"

"Maybe. Who were you listening to?"

"Sometimes it's my Guides or Angels. Sometimes my Higher Self or Mother Mary. It just depends on who shows up."

"Mother Mary as in Jesus' Mother?"

She nodded.

I told her about my own connection to La Virgen Maria and how she had become my favorite saint. "I was afraid you'd think I was nuts if you knew that."

My mother laughed. "Oh, baby, I've got a lot more crazy than that to tell you about."

CHAPTER FIFTY-FIVE

It took an hour for my mother to tell me the entire story. Her second marriage was to a man named Paul, who was a first-class jerk. I was shocked to learn that my mother had attempted suicide after she learned of Paul's infidelities. I couldn't picture this strong woman being so broken that she thought there was no hope for the future.

She told me about the supernatural event that saved her life.

"Wait a minute. That's impossible. You're telling me a ghost woke up Marci and told her to call you."

My mother nodded. "I swear that's what happened. When she couldn't reach me on the phone, she drove over to my house and found me comatose from an overdose."

She was so matter of fact about it, like she was telling me about a bad haircut or finding a rotten apple in the bottom of the bag.

She must have noticed the look on my face. "I'm not ashamed of how far I fell, Evie. I will shout it from the rooftops if it helps just one person recover from the guilt and shame of a suicide attempt.

"Paul was murdered by the woman he had an affair with. He eventually dumped her, and she blamed me. Framing me for his murder was her revenge. Well, along with the other personalities who lived inside her head."

I stared at my mother. If I didn't know her to be absolutely scrupulous about telling the truth, I would swear she was making this up.

"Danny and Biz, his partner that you met at the house, thought I was guilty at first because the DNA evidence against me was solid. Eventually they figured out Abigail was responsible."

"How can you be so calm about this? You almost went to prison."

"I'm doing a lot better now. For a while I thought I was going crazy because I fell for Danny the first time I met him. And then after Abigail tried to kill me, I had terrible nightmares."

"What about you and Álvaro? How did you meet?"

I told my mother everything. "I think I fell in love with him when he bought me the Coke and pillow in Birmingham." My mother's eyes softened and she rubbed my arm when I told her about losing the baby.

"Oh darling, I am sorry. You must have been so scared." She teared up. "I am so thankful Álvaro was there for you. I'm so sorry I wasn't."

We sat there for a moment, me reliving that moment so long ago, and my mother full of regret that we did not have the kind of relationship then that would have allowed me to be truthful with her.

What my mother said next was the last thing I would have expected.

"Evie, can I do a Tarot reading for you?" She picked up the deck of Tarot cards and an embroidered silk bag. She dumped the contents of the bag into my hand.

"Crystals? You brought rocks with you?"

My mother shrugged. "I brought the things that are important to me."

Something gold glinted underneath the stones in my hand. A gold chain, with a tiny ring threaded through the links. It was my baby ring.

My mother took it out of my hand. "The day you left, I put this on a chain. I wear it every day." She opened the clasp and fastened it around her neck. "For the last twenty-six years, I've said a prayer every morning that you would somehow find your way back to me."

She wiped tears from her eyes. "And now, here you are." She looked around at our surroundings. "Wherever the hell this is."

CHAPTER FIFTY-SIX

When I was growing up, anything that was considered "occult" was not allowed by my parents. Scary movies and Ouija boards were forbidden.

Halloween was a nightmare for me. I didn't have permission to go to the haunted houses with my friends (of course, I went anyway). My trick or treat costumes were Bible characters. Yeah, *Bible characters.*

Every year I wore a white sheet toga and went as Miriam, Moses' sister, or Mary, Jesus' mother, or Ruth, Boaz's wife. One year I was very excited to dress up like Queen Esther. I got to wear a cardboard crown spraypainted gold and sprinkled with glitter and plastic rhinestones.

I'm not certain which alternate universe I've entered in which my mother, former Methodist pastor's wife, and current psychologist, is reading Tarot cards for me.

Placing the Tarot deck in my hands she said, "Close your eyes and set your intention to hear from your Higher Self and Guides."

Okaaaay. . .

She took the deck from me and counted out cards, laying three cards from different parts of the deck face down on the table. She turned the first one over.

"The High Priestess. Obviously, that's you. You are being asked to trust yourself, your own divine wisdom, and develop your powers of intuition. Connect to your Higher Self; the answers you seek are within you." She paused and looked at me. "Does that resonate with you?"

Maybe. I had been beating myself up for not following the plan Álvaro and I had agreed to. I had begun calling the damn plan *The Stupid Set In Stone Damned If You Deviate From It Plan.* But only to myself.

Now a new thought formed in my mind. What if it was my intuition that had guided me to send Azul to Atlanta alone? *What if that was the plan and it happened the way it was supposed to?* Hmm, definitely something to ponder.

She turned over the second card.

"King of Pentacles. Yes, that's Álvaro, of course. This represents a person who is generous, a disciplined and successful business leader, with high ambition."

That was certainly my husband. Was there anything about being stubborn as a burro in that card?

I gasped when I saw the third card. A man was laying on the ground with a lot of knives stuck in his back. Yep, that's just how this last week has felt.

"Interesting, Ten of Swords. Now, this looks like a very frightening card, but it's not."

"Really? Because that man sure looks dead to me."

"No, this card is about the end of a struggle and new beginnings." She picked up the card. "See the yellow on the horizon? That's a new dawn." She cocked her head like she was listening. "Everything you've been through has been for a reason. You've learned the lessons you were supposed to." She looked at me and smiled. "You and Álvaro are starting a beautiful new chapter of your lives."

I breathed a silent prayer to my personal saint, La Virgen. *Please let that be one single chapter together and not two separate chapters heading in opposite directions.*

CHAPTER FIFTY-SEVEN

The clang of the iron bar lifting on the door startled us. Naja carried two brown paper bags into the room. I didn't realize how hungry I was until I caught a whiff of hamburgers and French fries. "There are drinks in the refrigerator." He indicated the mini fridge in the corner.

As he turned to leave, he said, "Good news, ladies, Señor Salas will see you at 9:00 sharp tomorrow morning." He shut the door firmly and we heard the locks click into place.

We dug into the food. "Oh, this is an amazing burger." I rooted around in the bags. "Yum, two each." I dumped what looked like enough fries to feed an army onto the table.

"I wonder what the guys are doing right now."

"They are worrying about us. They must be frantic. I hope Danny doesn't do anything stupid."

"Like what?"

"Like call in the cavalry. I think we are in a safe house somewhere, apart from El Tiburón's usual haunts. I hope after our meeting tomorrow morning we can make contact with Álvaro and get this resolved before Danny has time to put together a raid and annihilate everything in his path."

"He really loves you, doesn't he?"

"Yes, he does, and I love him back. I finally found my Twin Soul."

"That's what Álvaro calls us! *Almas Gemelas*, Twin Souls." I told my mother about our life in Taxco, my success as a silversmith, and how Álvaro had grown our business into a large wholesale operation.

"That's amazing. You know, I believe there are no mistakes in life. We often meet our destiny on the road we took to avoid it."

I smiled. "Jean de La Fontaine. My therapist told me the same thing." I told my mother about Isabella and how, as part of my therapy, she had given me a copy of *Love Hungry* to read.

"Really? What did you think of it?"

"Honestly, I wondered where the woman who wrote that book was when I needed her."

My mother was solemn. I looked for traces of anger in her face. There was none; only sorrow.

"You had every right to think that. Your leaving was my watershed moment. I took a long look at myself and admitted that I had completely failed you. I made a choice to become a different person."

I took my mother's hand. "You realize how ironic it is that neither of us would have become the people we are today without the way things happened."

"I do, love. You are one of my greatest teachers. Do you know one of my favorite mottos?"

I grinned. "Let me guess. 'There is no good. There is no bad. There are only teachers.'"

My mother laughed. "Oh yeah, you read the book."

CHAPTER FIFTY-EIGHT

There were no windows in our room and our phones had been confiscated by Naja. Neither I nor my mother had worn watches, so we had no idea of the time. However, our bodies were telling us it was time to rest.

The bathroom was spacious and outfitted like a fancy hotel bath. I wondered what this space was used for when it wasn't kidnapping season.

My mother looked worn out. I mentally calculated her age. If I recalled her birthdate correctly, she would be in her mid-sixties. If I was tired, my mother had to be absolutely exhausted. I laid out her pajamas while she showered (Surprise! It's a tee shirt and leggings) and turned down her side of the bed.

I tucked the sheet around her and then joined her in the king-size bed.

"Mom?"

"Yes."

"I love you."

"I love you back, Evie."

CHAPTER FIFTY-NINE

W e slept like the dead until Naja banged on the door. He brought us another round of Starbucks lattes and scones. "Señor Salas will see you in fifteen minutes."

We jumped out of bed and dressed quickly. My mother scrubbed her face and applied moisturizer. She ran her hands through her hair, applied some kind of waxy stuff, and scrunched it. She was ready in five minutes. *Alternate Universe, I reminded myself.* Either that or my mother has been abducted by aliens and this was a pod person.

My mother sat calmly sipping her latte and eating a scone while I rushed around the room getting ready.

"Evie."

I paused my frenzy for a moment.

My mother came to my side and held her fingertips to my temples. "Breathe. In and out. Breathe in peace. Breathe out stress. In and out. Everything will be OK."

"You don't know that."

She whispered in my ear.

"The High Priestess always trumps The Devil."

CHAPTER SIXTY

I was shocked when I saw El Tiburón. He was nothing like I expected. At one time he had been the most dangerous *jefe* in all of Mexico. *El mero mero*. The man before me was a shrunken wrinkled shell, sitting in a wheelchair and breathing oxygen from a cannister. Naja stood behind him. *El teniente*. The lieutenant.

When he spoke, there was still a vestige of the power he once wielded. "Señora Castillo," he stretched a wobbly hand toward me. "I am pleased to meet you." His voice was strong and forceful. He was a man yet to be feared.

He turned to my mother. "Dr. Cassidy. It is a pleasure. You have a lovely daughter." He gestured to the chairs in front of him. "*Por favor*, sit."

I was incredulous. The man spoke like he was inviting us to join him in a cup of tea. Perhaps my mother was right, and we were not going to be killed. I relaxed a little.

El Tiburón tapped Naja's sleeve. Naja placed the oxygen mask over El Tiburón's mouth and nose. He took several deep breaths. Naja removed the mask when El Tiburón tapped his sleeve again.

"You must be wondering why you are here." The man made an attempt to smile. His teeth were yellowed with age. He had to have been in his nineties, at least.

"My name is Pedro Luis Salas. You, Señora Castillo, are married to my son, Juan."

"What? No, that's not true. My husband's name is Álvaro. He is not your son."

"Juan doesn't know he is my son."

"His name is not 'Juan.' It's Álvaro Castillo. His father abandoned him when he was eight. You are mistaken."

"I am sorry to be the one to tell you this, but your husband's name is not Álvaro Castillo. That is the *seudónimo* he chose when he left my employment."

That is not a word I was familiar with. Naja explained, "Álvaro Castillo is an alias, *Señora.*"

"My son's—your husband's—birthname is Juan Alarcón Lopez. He believed Manuel Alarcón was his father. He was not. He was his stepfather." Señor Salas tapped Naja's sleeve again. He needed more oxygen. We waited.

I started to protest again but my mother held my arm. "Let's hear what Mr. Salas has to say, Evie."

"Juan's mother was the prettiest girl in Chilpancingo. Everyone, including me, courted her. It was Manuel who won Evangelina's heart. He didn't know she was already pregnant with my child when they married." The man sighed, as if the memories were weighing him down. He struggled to breathe.

"She loved Manuel, but she needed my money. One day, Manuel caught us together. Before I could intervene, he struck Evangelina so hard that it broke her neck." He hung his head.

"The same day, he took Juan and Maria Luisa to another town and left them. I never found out where he took them. I threatened to kill him if he didn't tell me. Manuel just laughed and walked away. One of Lina's brothers killed him in retaliation. I believed I would never see our son and daughter again.

"But many years later, *un milagro* occurred. One of my sons was at university with Juan. They became friends. Diego asked if he could bring his poor orphaned friend home to stay with us over the summer. I recognized Juan right away. He looked just like my father as a young man.

"One thing led to another, and he eventually came to work for me." Señor Salas smiled. "I knew he was a DEA agent and that is why he agreed to work for me. He did not do much damage to my organization. Hector and I gave him disinformation for the most part."

"You knew Álvaro was DEA? Is that why you killed Maria Luisa? Is that why you want him dead?" I asked pointedly.

"Of course not. I would not do that to my son or my daughter. One of Hector's men killed Maria Luisa in retaliation for Juan killing Hector."

"I don't believe you. Mario Villa said you put a three-million-dollar bounty on Álvaro.

"It was not a bounty. It was *una comisión*, a finder's fee. I would never hurt any of my children."

I was struggling to comprehend what this man was saying. "I don't believe you. My husband is a good person. He cannot be your son."

"I have many sons, Señora Castillo." He patted Naja's hand. "They are all fine people."

The man went into a coughing fit. Naja gave him more oxygen.

"Why are we here, Mr. Salas?" my mother asked, her voice softer than mine would have been.

"I knew that if I attempted to meet with Juan, it would be a confrontation in which one or both of us would be killed. I believe you, *Señora*, can broker a meeting between me and my son without any harm coming to either of us.

"I want to see my son and my grandson before I die. You can make that happen, Mija."

El Tiburón started coughing again. Naja pushed his wheelchair toward one of the other rooms opposite ours. "Señor Salas needs his rest. Chaco?" He motioned for Chaco to herd us back into our room.

"I'm not your hija!" I shouted as Chaco pushed us into the room.

CHAPTER SIXTY-ONE

I was so angry I couldn't sit still. I paced around our room, throwing pillows and punching the upholstered chairs.

The door flung open and Naja stomped in. "You upset my father, *Señora*. He is a very ill man who just wants to see his son and grandson before he dies."

I rushed Naja, lowering my shoulder and hitting him square in the chest. I bounced off him, falling back on my ass. He didn't move an inch when I hit him.

"My husband is a good person! He is kind and honest and loyal! He is nothing like you or that drug-dealing scumbag."

Naja's face turned beet red, and his mouth narrowed into a tight angry line. He clenched and unclenched his fist several times.

"Go ahead, hit me, you bastard." I pummeled his chest.

"I will not hit my brother's wife," he said quietly, and left the room.

I collapsed on the bed in tears. It would kill Álvaro to know that El Tiburón, a man who was responsible for a major drug trafficking network and many deaths, was his father. When he had worked for the Morelia cartel, it was not because he wanted to. He was undercover at the behest of the DEA.

A horrible thought occurred to me. What if that were not true? What if Álvaro had only said he was working for the DEA so that my mother would not think I had married a drug dealer. Oh God, I didn't know what was true and what was a lie any longer. I felt like I was losing touch with reality.

CHAPTER SIXTY-TWO

Until now I had held my temper, reacted rationally to a possibly permanent breach in my marriage, and maintained my composure while being kidnapped and imprisoned.

Señor Salas' revelations, or lies, whichever they are, were too much for me. My mother tried to comfort me, but I couldn't stop crying. I was hyperventilating and started throwing up.

My mother banged on the door. Chaco opened it. "Bring me a cup of tea and some pastries or donuts or something. NOW," she shouted.

Chaco moved to close the door. "And leave the blasted door open!" She pulled a chair over and propped the door open.

She came to my side and held me. She didn't try to shush me. She didn't offer meaningless platitudes. She simply held me, her presence a calming oasis of tranquility in the midst of my roiling emotions.

I don't know how long it was before Chaco scurried in with two mugs of tea and some saltine crackers. When my mother placed the warm mug into my hand, my soul quieted and my anxiety along with it. We sat on the floor together, our backs against the bed while I composed myself.

"You are stronger than you think. I just saw a bad ass take on the head of a drug cartel with no fear." My mother pulled me against her shoulder.

"What if what he said is true?" I whispered.

"All right. Let's process this. If it is true, what does that mean to you?"

"It means my son's grandfather is a horrible person. I can't ever let him know that's his heritage."

"Azul doesn't ever have to know that Salas is his grandfather. That is something for you and Álvaro to decide."

"My poor Álvaro."

"You really think he doesn't know?"

I nodded my head. "I think he believes the man who abandoned him and Maria Luisa is his father. Although, come to think of it, I never knew his parents' names. He told me his mother died when he was eight years old and that his father put them on the streets shortly afterward. He never called them by name. I assumed the family name was Castillo.

"He and Maria Luisa lived on the streets for a while begging for food and sleeping under overpasses until a church orphanage took them in.

"I need to lay down. I'm exhausted."

My mother kissed my forehead. "Sounds like a good plan. I'm going to ask Naja if he will let me use a phone to call Danny. He and Biz could come barreling in here any minute. I'm going to ask Álvaro to come here and meet with his father."

"Please don't call him that. He's a monster, not my father-in-law."

CHAPTER SIXTY-THREE

I was exhausted, nauseated, and my head was pounding. But I couldn't sleep. I tossed and turned for a few minutes and then went looking for my mother and something for my aching head.

She was sitting in a chair, talking on the phone. Naja was sitting beside her. She was wrapping up a conversation. I assumed it was with Danny.

"Ok, we'll see you in thirty minutes. Call this number when you are here and Naja will escort you in."

Naja pulled a chair over for me. He brought me a Coke and some medicine.

"It's a good thing I contacted Danny. SWAT was almost ready to launch an assault on this building. Danny has ordered them to stand down temporarily until Álvaro can speak with Mr. Salas."

My mother turned to Naja. "Make certain Mr. Salas understands that Álvaro will be armed, and that SWAT will have the building surrounded.

Naja nodded. "We accept those terms." He turned to me, "It will be good to see my brother again."

"Álvaro knows you are his brother?"

"No. I have always known, but he did not. You ladies should pack your bags. You'll be leaving after Juan and my father talk.

"*Con su permiso*. Excuse me, I must make certain my father is awake and ready to greet his prodigal son."

CHAPTER SIXTY-FOUR

Naja wheeled Señor Salas into the open area. The man did not look well. He was paler than before and taking oxygen more often. He seemed on the brink of death. I wondered if he would last until Álvaro arrived.

I sat in the chair beside him and put my hand on his. His skin was so thin and papery. "Señor Salas, I want to apologize for being rude to you earlier. Please forgive me."

He patted my hand so lightly it felt as if a butterfly was fluttering over it. He had no strength left. Under ordinary circumstances, I would have had pity for a man this fragile. But I had made a call to my friend Ashley's home a few days ago. I had promised her I would keep in touch, but I hadn't. Ashley's mother, Mrs. Thompson, answered the phone.

"Sweetheart, Ashley died twenty years ago. An overdose. Heroin."

How had my best friend, a girl I'm certain never used drugs when I knew her, become a junkie in her twenties?

"It was that boy she was seeing. Jett. He came home from college after that terrible injury playing, what was it? Some kind of sport. He got her hooked on drugs. They both were.

"They died together, you know. We found them in Ashley's apartment." Mrs. Thompson broke down. "The needles were still in their arms." She sobbed for a while. Then, "Who did you say this is, honey? Did you know my Ashley?"

El Tiburón had controlled most of the drug trade in Atlanta since the early 1970s. I'd bet my life it was his poison in the syringes that killed Ashley and Jett.

I hung up the phone sick to my stomach. If I had stayed in Atlanta with Jett, would that have been my fate, too?

El Tiburón sighed. "I was not always the man I am now. When I was very young, I dreamed of being a priest." He must have seen the startled look on my face. "*De veras*. It's true. But my family was very poor, and we could not pay the church to train me. I was angry. With God and with the church.

"I never darkened the doors of a church again. I started running alcohol, mescal and tequila. And then we started growing *la mota*, marijuana, and the business grew from there. Soon *los Colombianos* joined us with *la coca* and, well, *aquí estamos*. Here we are." His hand fluttered over mine again. "But you have no interest in the memories of an old man."

"Do you regret the sorrow you have brought to so many families whose lives have been destroyed by the drugs you sold?"

The man's eyes were red rimmed and cloudy. "*Querida*, I have so many regrets. More than I can count. I hope God will forgive me. I think He will if I make peace with Juan before I die."

We heard the sirens approaching. It was thunderous; it sounded like the entire precinct was descending on the building. I heard the rotors of a helicopter hovering overhead.

My mother answered the ringing phone in her hand. "Naja will open the garage door. Álvaro, only you are to enter. Confirm, please."

Naja looked at my mother. She nodded. He opened the door.

Álvaro came in with a gun in his hand. He looked around and when he saw me, he holstered it and ran to my side. Naja closed the door.

Álvaro lifted me off my feet. "*Gracias a Dios*. Are you hurt? Are you OK? Evita, *te quiero, mi amor*." He put me down and reached for my mother. "*Señora*, are you OK?"

"I'm fine, Álvaro. We're fine. We were not hurt."

Álvaro nodded to Naja. "Let Eva and Señora Cassidy leave. I will stay."

Naja shook his head. "No, 'mano, they stay."

Álvaro removed his cell phone and dialed. "Danny, both of them are A-OK, but Salas won't let them leave. We'll be coming out together. I'll keep you advised."

My husband had never used the phrase "A-OK" in his life as far as I knew. That must have been a code word established to confirm we had not been harmed, to keep all hell from breaking loose.

Señor Salas spoke softly. "Juan. *Vete aquí, hijo.*" Come here, son.

Álvaro approached him. "The years have not been kind to you, Pedro Luis. You're halfway in the grave."

Salas managed a small smile. "*Es la verdad. Acércate.* That's true. Come closer."

Álvaro sat in the chair closest to El Tiburón. He had to lean in and put his ear close to the man's mouth to hear his words. It was a surreal tableau; they seemed to be reminiscing and exchanging pleasantries.

I couldn't hear what was being said, but I could tell by the expressions on my husband's face the moment Salas revealed he was his father.

Álvaro recoiled in horror. His face fell and looked like he wanted to punch the man.

"No! *¡Eso es imposible! ¡Mentiras!* Lies!" Álvaro shook his head. "My mother would never be with a man like you."

Salas motioned for Naja to come closer. He whispered in Naja's ear. Naja reached under the blanket on his lap and withdrew a tattered envelope. Naja handed the envelope to Álvaro.

Álvaro opened the envelope and withdrew the letter. I could see tears streaming down his face as he read it.

I was uncomfortable watching my husband suspended in such agony. My mother stood beside me with her eyes closed, gripping my hand tightly. I saw her lips moving but she wasn't making any sound. Maybe she was doing some of her voodoo.

Álvaro held out the letter to me. I took it. At the top was the date: November 11, 1980.

Dearest Pebo, I love you with all my heart, but you must understand why I will not marry you, even though I am carrying your child. The life you live is full of danger. I do not want such a life for my children or myself. Manuel has asked for my hand, and we are to be married on Saturday. I will always love you more, Lina.

CHAPTER SIXTY-FIVE

My mother opened her eyes and cleared her throat. "If I may?"

She put her hand on my husband's shoulder. "You've had a great shock. Let's sit for a moment with Mr. Salas and talk about why he has brought you here."

"I don't want anything to do with him."

"Please, honey, just sit here," she said gently. I could tell my mother was in 'therapist mode.' Álvaro acquiesced and let my mother guide him to the chair beside El Tiburón. She motioned for me to sit with them.

"Mr. Salas, it is no secret that you are dying. I gather there are some things you want to say to Álvaro?" El Tiburón nodded.

"Álvaro, can you listen to what Mr. Salas has to say? It's up to you. No one is forcing you."

Álvaro sat stiffly in the chair, stone-faced.

"Mr. Salas, what do you want to say to Álvaro?"

Naja removed Salas' oxygen mask. At this point when he wasn't talking, he had the mask over his nose and mouth. He was getting weaker by the minute.

"Evangelina was the love of my life. I loved you and your sister. I tried to find you after Manuel sent you and Maria Luisa away."

Álvaro shifted in his seat. "Do not say their names with your filthy mouth." He balled up his fists.

Naja moved like he was going to restrain Álvaro, but Salas stayed him. "I need your forgiveness, *mijo.*"

Álvaro laughed scornfully. "I needed a father. And a mother. It looks like neither of us will ever have what we need." He turned to me. "We're done here. Let's go."

My mother and I retrieved our bags from the room. "What will happen now?" I whispered to my mother.

"Not a thing until we are safely away from here. After that, if I know Danny and Biz, all hell will break loose."

Álvaro made the call to notify Danny we were coming out. Naja accompanied us to the garage door. "When I open the door, take a step outside and stop. Do not move until the door is completely closed."

We did as we were told. When the door hit the ground, Danny rushed toward my mother. She flew into his arms.

Álvaro and I supported each other as we were escorted to a waiting police vehicle. "Where is Zuzu?"

"He's with Marci. He's worried about you. I told him Grandpa and I would bring you home safe." In the backseat of the police car, Álvaro covered me with kisses. Azul's teddy bear was in the pocket on the back of the front seat. "Azul sent Chico for you, in case you were scared."

As we drove away, I heard ear-splitting explosions. I looked back. The garage door had been breached and was in shreds. SWAT was swarming into the building with Danny and Biz close behind them.

My mother was in the front passenger seat. She turned around and reached for Álvaro. "Thank you, *mijo*. I love you."

The dam broke and I sobbed uncontrollably. We were safe. But we would never be the same after this.

CHAPTER SIXTY-SIX

Azul dashed out of my mother's house when he heard our car in the driveway. He hugged me tightly with a strength I didn't know he had. He took my face in his little hands and said, "I was so scared when the bad men took you, Mami."

I sat on the front steps and pulled him into my lap. "I was, too, Zuzu, but Grandma helped me be very brave." My mother sniffled behind me.

"I love Grandpa and Grandma, Mami. Can we stay here with them?" I heard my mother let out a sob.

Marci came out to the porch with her hands on her hips. "I've got a pan of lasagna in here that's getting cold. Hustle up, people."

She shooed everyone but my mother inside. "Jesus, Mary, and Joseph, Cal, what the hell is it with you and dangerous criminals. You're a psycho-magnet."

My mother laughed through her tears. "It comes with the job, Marce."

Marci snorted. "Well, then you need a new job. I can't take any more of this. Come on, let's eat."

We stuffed ourselves with lasagna. The conversation around the table was light—we did not want to upset Azul with any details of our ordeal.

Danny came in as we were finishing up the meal. Marci asked if she could take Azul to her restaurant. "We have some very special cupcakes to bake, and we didn't have time to do it before you came home." I loved that Azul's world was expanding beyond me and Álvaro. We had been very insular in Taxco, having only a few friends with children at Azul's school, and a few employees we were close to. Here, in my mother's world, we had family. Not just my mother and Danny, but Marci and Biz.

The four of us sat around the table with coffee and a blueberry tart Marci had brought over from Serendipity.

"Is everyone in custody?"

"No. El Tiburón is dead. Everyone else escaped."

"How the hell did anyone escape? You had the building surrounded. Plus air cover."

"As soon as you two were safe," Danny nodded to me and my mother, "we went in. Salas was slumped over in his wheelchair. Looks like he died of natural causes, but the coroner will have to confirm that."

"Where were the rest of them?"

"Originally that building was an automotive garage. There were underground pits for changing oil. Those pits had been expanded into tunnels. By the time we discovered the tunnels, Naja and his men were long gone."

Álvaro asked Danny, "When we can get an updated assessment about the threat level for my family?"

"An official report will take a week or so. I'm certain we eliminated the immediate threat this morning. We had an informant inside the organization. His last report indicated El Tiburón had transferred power to Naja a few months ago."

I was curious. "What is the informant's name?"

"Carlos. They called him, 'Chaco.'"

"Chaco!" My mother and I laughed. We told Danny and Álvaro the witch story. I told Danny how brave my mother had been and how she had handled the entire situation with levelheadedness.

"She has a way of doing that when she's under pressure," Danny smiled and hugged my mother. They had a good thing going. I was thankful she had found someone who loved and appreciated her.

"If Naja is now *El Jefe*, I think we're safe."

"How so?" asked Álvaro.

I recounted the conversations I'd had with El Tiburón. Danny's eyes widened in surprise when he learned that

Salas was Álvaro's father and Naja his half-brother. "Mom had it figured out fairly early. We were kidnapped so that Salas could open a line of communication with you, Álvaro. El Tiburón was fearful that a meeting with you would end in bloodshed if it were not carefully arranged.

"We were wrong about El Tiburón being a threat to us. He was a dying old man who just wanted to talk to his son one last time."

Álvaro shook his head. "I don't know how to reconcile that. I can't. Not yet anyway."

Danny reached over and put his hand on my husband's shoulder. "Son, we'll get through this together. "

"So will you go back to Mexico, or will you go to Canada?"

My mother's question was valid, but Álvaro and I hadn't discussed our next steps. I knew where my heart was leading, but I needed to discuss it with Álvaro first.

"Well," said Álvaro, smiling, "I have not discussed this with Eva, but I think Azul needs to get to know his grandparents better." He kissed my hand. "I think we might stay here a while."

"Yes!" I shouted.

Danny was nodding his head. They both had huge smiles on their faces at the thought of their only grandchild being close by.

"Can you afford that?" my mother asked.

Álvaro and I laughed. "We have a rather large international company that wholesales Eva's silver designs. We own a home in Taxco and another in Canada. The Canadian home was part of our escape plan, which we don't need now. Maybe we'll sell that one and buy one here."

"Well in that case, Danny, I think it's time for us to retire and become full-time grandparents." My mother grabbed my hand and squeezed it. "We have a lot of lost time to make up for."

Just then Azul and Marci marched through the door with a plate full of cupcakes. The cupcakes had about two inches of frosting and were smothered in chocolate chips and rainbow sprinkles.

Azul put the cupcakes on the table. "I decorated these all by myself," he said proudly. One by one he took the cupcakes off the plate and distributed them. He put two in front of his chair. "Marci said the chef always gets two," he said solemnly, as if this was a law we could not dispute.

His little face was beaming as he picked up one of the cupcakes and took a huge bite. It left remnants of frosting on both cheeks and his nose.

Álvaro and I leaned over to kiss those little chocolate-covered cheeks at the same time.

CHAPTER SIXTY-SEVEN

We decided to stay in the AirBnb we had originally intended to be a safe house. Why not? We all needed a little vacation. The events of the last few days had left us emotionally and physically exhausted.

The house had two master suites, a pool, and tennis courts. For the first few days we lazed around the pool. My mother and Danny bought Azul all kinds of pool toys and they played with him non-stop while Álvaro and I relaxed. It didn't take long to reestablish our heart connection and we promised each other we would never let ourselves get so out of sync again.

Marci supplied us with more delicious food than we could eat in a month, and she stayed over with us a couple of nights. I forgot how much fun she was. She had been a part of my life since I was born, and it was good to reconnect with my "Auntie Marchie," as I called her when I was a baby.

Biz and her wife would come over after work and we played card games late into the night. Azul was an unbeatable Uno shark. Danny and Mom were into Pickle Ball. Álvaro and I tried to beat them, but the old goats were pros. We lost several bets before we caught on to their strategies. Marci was teaching Azul how to bake, and they made a different treat every day.

Life was good. No, life was *great*.

Danny took a phone call from the precinct early one morning. Afterward he gathered us around the breakfast table. "The coroner's office called. Mr. Salas died of natural causes. The coroner needs to know what to do with his body."

Álvaro didn't hesitate. "I don't care."

"I understand, son. That means he will be buried in a pauper's grave. Are you good with that?"

Álvaro sighed. "Where is Naja or any of Salas' other crew?"

"They've gone to ground. They are not at their usual haunts."

"What's the word on the street? Have you heard from Chaco?"

"Nobody knows anything. Chaco hasn't been in touch. He's overdue. We're a little worried."

"Do you know where your mother is buried?" I asked.

"Chilpancingo." This was a town south of Taxco, on the way to Acapulco.

"Think about honoring your mother. Would she want the man she truly loved to be buried beside her?"

"He didn't deserve her love."

"I know that, but sometimes we can't help who we love."

"Let me think about it." Álvaro left the table.

Later when I went into our room, Álvaro was lying on the bed staring at the ceiling. "I don't know what to do."

I lay beside him and put my hand on his heart. "Yes, you do, *mi amor*. Your heart knows what to do."

At dinner that night, Álvaro told us his decision. "I will take my father back to his birthplace and bury him beside my mother."

"I'm going with you." Álvaro shook his head, but I stopped him. "You are not going alone."

Danny whispered something to my mother, and she nodded. "Would you like for us to come along? We would like to visit Taxco and see where you live. But if that's an imposition, we understand."

Álvaro's face lit up. "That would be wonderful. I would like that very much."

My mother smiled. "We're family. You're stuck with us."

CHAPTER SIXTY-EIGHT

It turned out it wasn't going to be easy to get Salas' body back to Mexico through official channels. Danny contacted officials at the Mexican embassy who said it would take "six months, *más o menos*, more or less" to file the paperwork and make arrangements. Although, one official indicated for 800,000 pesos it could happen much sooner."

"How much is that in dollars?" my mother asked.

"Almost fifty thousand dollars," Álvaro said, shaking his head. "The corruption never ends."

"I might have a solution." Everyone looked at me expectantly. "Before we left Shark Camp, Naja gave me his mobile number." My mother and I referred to our time as El Tiburón's 'guests' as Shark Camp. Neither Álvaro nor Danny thought it funny. We thought it was hilarious. It was another one of those inappropriate responses to stressful situations that is in our DNA. The more I get to know my mother, the more I realize we, too, are *Almas Gemelas*, Twin Souls.

Danny stood up. "I need to excuse myself from this conversation. My job is to arrest that man, not make deals with him." He left the kitchen and set up a game of Uno with Azul in the family room.

Álvaro was incredulous. "Why would Naja give you his phone number?"

I shrugged. "My guess is he respects family ties. He's known all along that you're his brother. We're your family and that makes us his family, too."

"What are you suggesting?"

"I'm just thinking out loud. When you worked for Salas, did he have a private jet?"

"Yes, several."

"If the coroner released the body to a private funeral home, why couldn't Naja retrieve it and fly his father to Mexico? That would cost a lot less than fifty thousand dollars."

"That's a lot of ifs and maybes. And maybe not completely legal."

I held out my phone. "There's only one way to find out if it would work."

CHAPTER SIXTY-NINE

Four days later we were standing beside a freshly dug grave. Álvaro, my mother, Danny, Azul, and I had taken a commercial flight. Naja had transported Salas' body to Chilpancingo on his private jet.

Álvaro's mother had been buried long ago by her family in a small cemetery by the Huacapa River. Pedro Luis and Evangelina, who were separated in life, were finally reunited in death.

Two of Evangelina's sisters, and a handful of cousins he hadn't seen since he was eight years old, were in attendance. The family was overjoyed to be reacquainted with their long-lost nephew and cousin. They embraced me, my mother, and Danny as family. Of course, they fussed over Azul, and he was overjoyed with the attention of more *'tias* and *primos*, aunts and cousins.'

I caught a glimpse of Naja, standing beside a tree on the other side of the riverbank. I had told him over the phone, "Danny will have no choice but to arrest you if you are present at the funeral. It's his job, Naja, he cannot side-step the law." He understood and agreed to say his goodbyes at his father's gravesite after our departure. I raised my hand and waved when I saw him, standing tall and solemn beside the tree. He nodded in acknowledgment. I don't know if Danny saw him, but I appreciated the concession he made for his son-in-law.

After the interment, Evangelina's sister, Guadalupe, pulled me aside. She placed a small object in my hand. "This belonged to Evangelina. She loved her children dearly. It broke our hearts to lose our nephew and niece. Our brother, Reynaldo, killed Manuel in a fit of rage because he would not tell us where he had taken them. It was a tragic time for our family."

Guadelupe smiled. "God has seen fit to bring our Juan back to us. Along with his beautiful family." She embraced me and kissed me on the cheek. Of course, his family did not know my husband as 'Álvaro,' so we referred to him as 'Juan,' his birthname. There was no reason to create confusion or questions as to why 'Juan' had changed his name.

"Did your family know that Salas was Juan and Maria Luisa's father?"

"Yes." Guadalupe was somber. "Evangelina was our baby sister, and she was a wild child. We warned her about Pedro Luis; we knew what type of man he was. He was well established in the drug trade by the time she caught his eye. She was attracted to him like a moth to a flame. When she became pregnant, we finally convinced her that a life with him would be too dangerous for the child she was carrying.

"When Juanito was born, she tried to sever ties with Pedro Luis." Guadelupe sighed and shook her head. "Their love was *muy fuerte*, very strong. Nothing could break it. Who knows? Perhaps it was God's will that we were fighting against." She crossed herself. "*Gracias a Dios* that destiny brought them together again."

I opened my hand. A heavy antique silver charm in the shape of La Virgen Maria lay in my palm. It was exquisitely detailed and executed. I like to think all the prayers his aunts funneled through this little *milagro* kept my husband safe in his journey from childhood to today.

Life comes full circle. The entire *colonia* turned out to welcome Juan and his family home. A huge feast was prepared, and tables were set up in a park on the bank of the river. An iron cauldron sat on a large grate over a crackling fire. *Tamales*, elongated corn cakes wrapped in the husks, sat baking on the grate. I loved *tamales*, a typical southern Mexican dish. Some were filled with *chorizo*, a spicy pork sausage, some with cheese, and some with vegetables. Even though we had only been gone from Mexico a few weeks, I had missed the flavors, the landscape, and the ambiance of my home.

I took my turn stirring the fragrant stew in the cauldron. I pulled my hair back in *un panuelo*, a scarf, and put some muscle into stirring the stew thick with goat meat, hominy, chiles, and onion. It was, of course, *pozole*, which I have come to love.

I watched my mother and Danny interacting with Álvaro's family and community. They fit right in, even though they understood very little of what was being said. Azul stayed by their side, translating for his *abuela* and *abuelo*. Even though he was raised in Mexico, I made sure Azul was fluent in English. As a rule, we spoke English at home and Spanish everywhere else. Álvaro and I both agreed that we wanted Azul to have the advantage of being bilingual. One day he would inherit our international business and we knew it would be an advantage for him to know at least two languages.

After the *pozole* and *tamales*, plates of *flan*, a caramel-topped custard dusted with cinnamon, were brought out. Danny and my mother enjoyed the food with gusto. After dinner, while a mariachi band played traditional tunes, they danced under the starlight like the newlyweds they were.

Álvaro and I sat on a blanket, the grass cool and damp underneath our feet and a slight breeze blowing off the river. Danny was dancing with Azul in his arms and my mother was swaying around them, her skirt billowing in the breeze. I did not ever remember my mother enjoying life this much when she was married to my father. It made me happy to see her so happy.

Was it really less than a month ago that Mario appeared in Taxco and set into motion the events that would alter our lives? The choices and decisions we made momentarily shifted our path away from Taxco and guided us into the arms of both my family and Álvaro's family.

I held Evangelina's *milagro* in my hand and breathed a prayer of gratitude to La Virgen who had set each of our orbits around a singular sun. All our paths led us home.

CHAPTER SEVENTY

It was well past midnight when we left Chilpancingo and headed to Taxco. It was a two-hour drive under good conditions. Late at night on a curvy highway, we didn't arrive home until almost 4:00 a.m.

Once we knew we were coming back to Taxco, I had Ximena get the crew that maintained our office to clean up the house. Otherwise, we would have walked into what looked like a crime scene with blood all over the floor and walls. I assured Ximena we were all in good health and that Álvaro and I would explain everything when we got home.

The house was clean and aired out when we arrived. We insisted my mother and Danny take the master suite. It was late and they were tired, so they didn't argue too strenuously.

We had built a swinging bed in our gazebo because we liked to spend the night under the stars. By the time we laid down, the sun was almost cresting the mountains.

I slid my hand into Álvaro's pajama bottoms. I was happy he had the same idea I had. "Remember the first night we slept out here?"

"How could I forget that, *querida?* When I feared that El Tiburón would surely kill you to exact revenge on me, it was the memory of that night that gave me hope. I did not believe that a love as strong as ours could be extinguished by evil."

I unbuttoned his pajama top and kissed his neck. I loved Álvaro's scent and tonight it was mixed with sweat and woodsmoke. I was heady with desire. Our bodies had always been in sync, and we moved in an ecstatic dance of tongues and fingers pleasing each other. Just as the sun peaked over the mountain and illuminated the gazebo with a burst of golden light, I mounted him, and we came together in a crescendo of passion.

Drifting off to sleep, we were serenaded by the morning birds that built nests in our courtyard trees. It seemed they were singing, *"I am my beloved's, and my beloved is mine."*

CHAPTER SEVENTY-ONE

Around noon, my mother and Azul brought a pot of coffee and *postres* to us in the gazebo. "Mami! I showed Grandpa where to buy the *postres* and I helped Grandma make the coffee!"

I took a sip of coffee and a bite of the pastry. "Mmm, it's perfect, *piquito*. You are growing up so fast." He climbed on the bed with us.

My mother sat in a rocking chair beside the swing. "What does '*piquito*' mean? It sounds so cute."

"It literally means 'little beak.' When Azul was a baby, his little lips looked like the perfect little bird beak."

"That's adorable. Do you remember my nickname for you when you were a tiny baby?"

"No, I don't."

"When I held you after you were born, the first thing I noticed about you was your little mouth—it looked like a perfect little rose bud. I called you 'my little Rosy' for the longest time."

Álvaro touched my lips with his finger. "Rosita, how adorable. I love that." He got up from the swing and lifted Azul. "Come on, Zuzu. Let's get dressed and find Grandpa. I want to show him around town."

"Thank you for telling me that. I don't have a lot of memories of when I was little." What I actually meant was, I didn't have lot of good memories, but I didn't want to hurt my mother, so I didn't say that.

"That was a long time ago, Evie," she said, emphasizing 'long.' "I am thankful we have the opportunity to create new memories." She rose from her chair. "Let's go, Rosy. I want to see this amazing town of yours."

CHAPTER SEVENTY-TWO

We have lived in Taxco for twenty-seven years. When you live somewhere for that long, it is inevitable that you take things for granted. Walking around Taxco with my parents—yes, I had begun thinking of them that way—I saw my hometown in a new light. With fresh eyes I saw the splendor of the flower market. I recalled how as an eighteen-year-old aspiring artist I stood in the middle of the explosion of color and literally cried tears of joy.

My mother 'oohed' and 'ahhed' over so much in the Artisan's Market that I was certain Danny would have to get a U-Haul to carry everything home. We toured through Santa Prisca and my mother was suitably impressed by the pomp and circumstance of the art and décor. But, when I took her to the little rustic church where Álvaro and I committed our lives to one another, she sat in the pew and wept.

"Miracles have occurred here," she whispered, as she touched the hem of La Virgen's wooden robe. "This is a sacred place." I told her about the little old nun who told me, before I was pregnant, that I would have a son with blue eyes.

When I picked up Azul from school, we ran into Isabella. After giving her a brief update, "we had to unexpectedly leave town for a family emergency," I introduced her to my mother. Isabella was awestruck. She shook my mother's hand at least three times.

"Can the three of us have lunch together soon?" my mother asked. "I would love to have a chat with a fellow therapist." We arranged to meet the next day. Isabella later told me she didn't sleep a wink that night. She sat up all night perusing my mother's books, making notes of questions to ask her.

I had seen my mother in therapeutic mode when we were at Shark Camp. It was a new experience to watch her mentor a younger therapist. She was kind and open, welcoming all of Isabella's questions and answering them with honesty and even a bit of humble vulnerability. There was a moment when one of the 'if only' thoughts crossed my mind, but I practiced the exercise Isabella had taught me.

"When you are triggered and those old self-doubts and feelings pop up, it is a sign there is an unhealed part of you that is ready for healing. Go deep when that happens, Eva. The trigger is a gift." The irony of the trigger popping up while my therapist, Isabella, was talking to my mother, was not lost on me.

That night after I put Azul to bed, I broached the subject with my mother. "Remember when Isabella was asking you for advice about treating a patient whose parents are alcoholics, and you were listening with such focused attention that you didn't notice your cell phone ringing?" My mother nodded. "That triggered me."

My mother put down her cup of tea, aligned her body with mine until we were knee to knee, and made direct eye contact. "Tell me about that. How did you feel?"

"I remembered all the times I had something I felt was important that I needed to tell you, and for the most part, you were distracted during our conversations, paying attention to other people and things, and I never felt fully heard."

My mother sighed. "For the most part, your memories are accurate, my love. And I am so, so sorry. My priorities were not what they should have been. I should have put you first. Always. I didn't, and I regret it. Can you forgive me?"

"I have. When Álvaro and I started our business and it took off within a few years, we could hardly keep up with the growth. I remember thinking at the time I was thankful we did not have children because I would have been so torn between my ambition as a silversmith and artist and my role as a mother. No offense, but I don't think I would have handled things any better than you did."

We both chuckled. "You are a remarkable person, Eve." She took my hands in hers. "Thank you for the grace that you have shown me. It has healed years of my shame and guilt."

"Mom, do you think Dad died of a broken heart because I ran away?"

"No, love. I don't. Your father had a congenital heart condition that went undetected until he died. You were in no way responsible for his death."

Danny and Álvaro came in just then from a stroll downtown to *La Pastelería*. They smelled of coffee and cigars. Danny's cheeks were flushed, and they looked excited about something.

"I gotta tell you, I could get used to this life. Babe, did you see the house over on Cuauhtémoc that is for sale while you were walking around today?"

"Is that Beto's house?" I asked Álvaro. Our beloved Alberto Morejón had died in 2013 and one of his sons returned to Taxco to live in the house. We had heard from a neighbor that Victor had accepted a job at the Museo Nacional de Antropoligía and would be moving to Mexico City soon.

"Yes, it's Beto's house." Álvaro looked like the cat who swallowed the canary.

"What are you two up to? Spill the *frijoles*."

"Álvaro spoke with a notary today about buying the house. We have an appointment to look at it tomorrow at 11:00 a.m."

I clapped my hands. "Mom, you will love Beto's house!"

"I also spoke with Victor," said Álvaro. "He is selling all of the furniture with the house."

I looked at my parents. "Can you afford that?"

"I think so," said my mother. "I've written a few popular books."

CHAPTER SEVENTY-THREE

Of course, my parents loved Beto's house and of course, they bought it. Mom retired from teaching and Danny retired from the police department.

The day they closed on the house, I brought over *mole poblano* and *empanadas de calabasa* for dinner. I told them about the day we met Beto and the meal we shared that night. To my surprise, the Frida Kahlo painting was still hanging on the wall in an alcove. "Victor was kind enough to leave the painting with us, but Mr. Morejón's family retains ownership of it. He said it belongs in this house, and as long as we live here, the painting will as well."

After dinner, while Álvaro and Azul served coffee and *Pastel de Tres Leches,* I gave my mother a housewarming gift. She took the small 4" by 4" box and shook it. It jingled. "What could it be?" she mused. "A book? A pillow? A mirror?"

She unwrapped the box and peeked inside. "Oh, how beautiful. I love it."

It was the first bracelet I had made in many years. "I chose the charms specifically for you: a lotus, a hamsa, La Virgen Maria, a peace symbol, a wire wrapped crystal point, and six hearts that represent our family."

"Six? Am I getting a granddog?"

Azul was excitedly jumping up and down. I smiled. "Zuzu, would you like to tell Tito and Tita our surprise?"

"A sister! I'm getting a sister!"

CHAPTER SEVENTY-FOUR

I thought my mother was going to faint. I almost did when I went to my doctor a week ago and she did a pregnancy test.

***

"How can this be? I'm almost forty-six."

"I see a lot of pregnancies in peri-menopausal women. I don't want you to worry. Everything looks good at this point. We'll keep a close eye on you and baby. . .um, do you want to know what it is?"

"Claro, qué sí."

"It's a girl, Eva. Azul will have a little sister."

***

We carried our coffee outside and sat in the courtyard of my parents' new house. My mother and Danny were thrilled, and just as excited as Álvaro and Azul had been when I told them.

I recalled a line from my mother's book, *'what is meant for you, will not pass you by.'* Maybe life is a combination of fate and destiny. Do we instinctively know the master plan for our lives and choose the paths that take us there?

I don't know the answer. I only know that tonight, under a blanket of stars with the Swan swimming across the Milky Way, I am happier than I have ever been in my life. I am with all my favorite people.

More Romantic Mystery from WildBlue Press

WildBlue Press, 2016

WildBlue Press, 2017

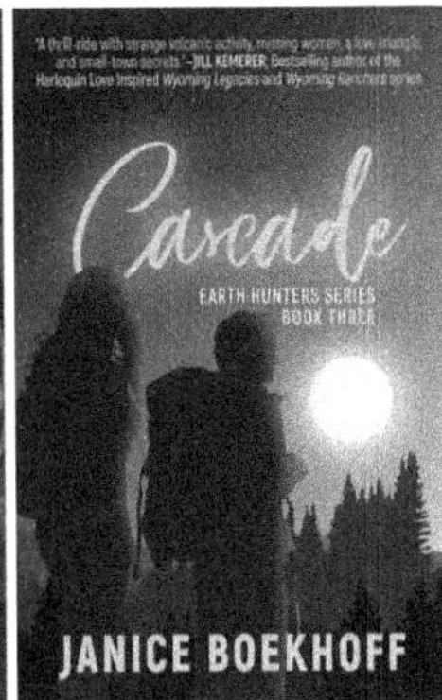

Lost Canyon Press, 2018

Janice Boekhoff's Earth Hunters Series embarks on captivating journeyes where ancient secrets reveal timless truths and pave the way to love and faith. These suspenseful blend heart-stirring adventure, romance, and wholesome themes.

In **CREVICE**, Elery Hearst delves into the depths of Arizona's Lost Dutchman's Mine. The quest for her family's legacy transforms into a soul-searching adventure, intertwining her fate with Lucan Milner. Together, they navigate a labyrinth of old wounds and emerging threats, their faith and emotions intensifying amidst the rugged terrain.

CREATED takes us to the lush, mysterious jungles of Costa Rica with Paleontology Professor Travis Perego. His pursuit of a revolutionary discovery challenges the boundaries between science and faith. Teaming up with Lenaia, a woman harboring her secrets, they face the wilderness, their ethical convictions, and their unresolved histories. In their journey, the struggle to safeguard their discoveries is as daunting as their quest for personal redemption.

In **CASCADE**, we meet Geologist Lenaia Talavera, who gets more than she bargained for when she's called to Mt. Rainier to investigate an act of sabotage. Not only is she forced to confront her left-over feelings for her ex-boyfriend—feelings her current boyfriend wouldn't appreciate—but women from the nearby town are disappearing… only to be found dead.

Unraveling these mysteries might not be easy, but it could be the key to a profound renewal of their lives and beliefs.